RED ZONE RIVALS

Also by Eric Howling
in the Lorimer Sports Stories series

Drive
Hoop Magic
Kayak Combat

RED ZONE RIVALS
Eric Howling

James Lorimer & Company Ltd., Publishers
Toronto

James Lorimer & Company Ltd., Publishers acknowledges the support of
the Ontario Arts Council. We acknowledge the financial support of the
Government of Canada through the Canada Book Fund for our publishing
activities. We acknowledge the support of the Canada Council for the Arts
which last year invested $24.3 million in writing and publishing throughout
Canada. We acknowledge the Government of Ontario through the Ontario
Media Development Corporation's Ontario Book Initiative.

Cover image: Shutterstock

Library and Archives Canada Cataloguing in Publication
Howling, Eric, 1956-, author
    Red zone rivals / Eric Howling.

(Sports stories)
Issued in print and electronic formats.
ISBN 978-1-4594-0714-5 (pbk.).--ISBN 978-1-4594-0715-2
(bound).--ISBN 978-1-4594-0716-9 (epub)

    1. Football--Juvenile fiction. I. Title. II. Series: Sports
stories (Toronto, Ont.)

PS8615.O9485R43 2014   jC813'.6   C2014-903023-1
C2014-903024-X

James Lorimer & Company Ltd., Publishers
317 Adelaide Street West, Suite 1002
Toronto, ON, Canada
M5V 1P9
www.lorimer.ca

Distributed in the United States by:
Orca Book Publishers
P.O. Box 468
Custer, WA, USA
98240-0468

Printed and bound in Canada.
Manufactured by Friesens Corporation in Altona, Manitoba, Canada in
August 2014.
Job #205573

For John and Joan

CONTENTS

1 COUNTDOWN

The clock ticked down.

There was less than a minute to play. The Riverbend Junior High Rebels trailed the Sprucewood Spartans 21–15 and needed a touchdown to win.

The ball sat deep in their own territory on the twenty-yard line. The field seemed to stretch out forever in front of them. Most of the players in the red uniforms thought the game was over. That their team had no chance to march eighty-five yards down the field and drive the ball over the Spartans' goal line. The Rebels' broke from their huddle and trudged to the line of scrimmage.

"Blue . . . forty-six . . . hut . . . hut!" Quinn Brown shouted out the signals for his team. He leaned over his stocky centre and waited for Braden Parker to snap the ball. On the final "hut" Quinn grabbed the pigskin from between Braden's legs and raced a few steps back.

Quinn's eyes flashed left looking for his receiver, but the Spartan defender was sticking to Carter Washington like glue. The Sprucewood pass rush was on. Two hulking linemen in black jerseys had broken through the Rebels' defensive line and were charging straight at him.

Quinn shifted gears and scrambled to his right. He scanned downfield searching for another receiver. There, breaking into the middle! Quinn cocked his arm and rifled a pass to Jordan Brooks, who was in the clear between the Spartan defenders. Jordan leaped high into the air to make the catch, tucked the leather under his arm, and dashed another ten yards before being tackled.

The Rebels had gained more than ten yards and the referee pointed downfield, signalling another first down. The ball lay on the forty-yard line. There were thirty-four seconds left. The Rebel players circled around Quinn in the huddle. He called the play — a square-out pass to his left wide receiver, Carter. Quinn hoped he'd be open this time.

"On two," Quinn barked, clapping his hands to break the huddle.

A ripple of hope spread through the Rebels. Legs were less heavy. Arms felt stronger. The twelve players jogged back to their positions on the line of scrimmage and waited for the snap.

"Eighteen . . . hut . . . hut!" On the second 'hut' Braden hiked the ball into Quinn's waiting hands. He backpedalled and watched Carter streak from the line of scrimmage. Quinn knew the square-out pattern was ten yards straight downfield and then a sharp left turn toward the sideline. He waited for Carter to cut, then threw the ball to his left just as he was turning. Carter ran three steps and the ball sailed right into his hands. *Complete!* He sprinted another twenty yards downfield before being brought down by the Spartans' safety.

The Rebels were on the move. The referee placed the ball on the Spartans' forty-yard line. They were in enemy territory. The clock showed twenty-two seconds. *Time for just two more plays*, Quinn thought to himself. What should those two plays be? He couldn't make a mistake. His team depended on him. His heart pounded. He started to panic. *How could a fourteen-year-old in grade nine know what to do?*

"Time out!" he shouted.

The referee in the zebra-striped shirt blew his whistle. Quinn ran to the sideline where Coach Gordon waited by the Rebels' bench.

His attention was sidetracked on the way. The Rebels cheerleading squad was in action. Each girl wore a red skirt and a long-sleeved white top with a big *R* across the front. The six girls stood in a line, clapping their hands and shouting the Rebels' cheer. "We are the Rebels . . . We can't be beat . . . Spartans watch out . . . Prepare for defeat!"

Quinn shot a glance at the head cheerleader and smiled. But this wasn't the time to think about his girlfriend, Emma. He had to focus on the game. Quinn snapped his eyes back to Coach on the sideline.

"Nice work!" Coach said.

"What do we do next?" Quinn said, throwing up his hands.

"Don't worry. You can do this."

Grady Gordon had coached the Rebels for twenty years. He had worn the same red Rebels hoodie and hat at every game, too. He wasn't the kind of coach to wear a suit and tie. Quinn had relied on him for the last two seasons. When Quinn panicked on the field, Coach knew how to calm him down. When Quinn didn't know what play to call, Coach knew exactly what to do. His brain was like a football computer. Quinn knew he'd have the answer for the last two plays of the game.

"We've got forty yards to go and only twenty-two seconds left," Coach Gordon said. He held a clipboard with all the play diagrams on it. "On the first play, let's run another square-out, but this time look for Jordan on the right side. He should be able to catch the ball and sprint out of bounds. That will stop the clock. Then we're going to try a running play."

Quinn's eyes widened. "Shouldn't we be passing the ball on the last play? We need a touchdown."

"That's exactly what the Spartans are going to expect," Coach said. "But we're not going to do what they expect. A running play will surprise them."

"Who should I give the ball to?" Quinn asked.

"Make the hand-off to Tank and he'll run straight up the middle to paydirt. You just wait and see."

Quinn had his doubts but he didn't have time to question Coach. The ref had blown his whistle to end the time out. Quinn trotted onto the field and headed back to his teammates, who were waiting for his instructions. Some players stood adjusting the tape on their beat-up hands while others knelt on the grass catching their breath. The Rebels were battered and bruised but their spirits were unbroken. They were ready to go.

2 CHANGE UP

Quinn looked around the huddle at the mud- and sweat-stained faces. "We can do this boys!" He used the same confident tone he had just heard from Coach Gordon. "Two plays and we're in for the score. The first is a square-out pass to Jordan. On three . . . and break!"

The Rebels gave a single thunderous clap of their hands and ran to the line of scrimmage. The Spartans dug their cleats into the chewed-up grass and waited for them.

"Hut one . . . hut two . . . hut three!"

Quinn squeezed the ball from Braden. Jordan bolted from the line and sprinted downfield. Quinn stepped back into the pocket formed by the linemen who guarded him against the oncoming rush.

The Spartans' front four were big, strong, and fast. They flooded through the Rebels' defence like water bursting through a crumbling dam. Four giants closed in on Quinn. The long arms of the tallest Spartan had a tight grip on his red jersey. Quinn twisted out of the

Spartan's grasp, sending him tumbling to the ground.

Quinn spun to his right, looked downfield, and spotted Jordan about to cut to the sideline. Just before being nailed by a second charging lineman, Quinn flicked his wrist and tossed a perfect fifteen-yard spiral into Jordan's outstretched hands. Jordan made the catch and dashed another fifteen yards down the sideline before the Spartans' defensive back pushed him out of bounds at the ten.

The ref blew his whistle to stop the clock. Quinn looked up at the scoreboard. Just five seconds left. They were in the red zone — just inside the twenty-yard line, where they had a good chance to score.

"Huddle up!"

The Rebels gathered around their quarterback. All eyes were on Quinn.

"This is our last play. We need to score. Tank — it's a hand-off to you, on one."

Quinn knew his teammates would wonder about the call. *A running play? What was that about?* Just like the Spartans, they were expecting another pass. They thought that was their only chance for a touchdown. But just like Quinn, every member of the Rebels trusted Coach Gordon. If Coach thought this was the right play, then this was the right play. Carter, Jordan, and the rest of the Rebels broke from the huddle and lined up, waiting for the ball to be snapped one last time.

After just a single "Hut!" Quinn took the quick

snap from Braden and dropped back as if he were going to pass. The Spartans came storming across the line with fire in their eyes. They raised their arms, expecting Quinn to throw the ball just as he had on every other play of the drive. The Rebel front line blocked the Spartans, forcing them to the sides and leaving a gaping hole in the middle of the field. That's when Quinn faked throwing the pass and handed the ball to Tank. Tommy "Tank" Taggert squeezed the pigskin to his gut with his pudgy hands, put his head down, and rumbled straight ahead.

The first five yards were easy. No one stood in Tank's way. Then he met a wall of Spartans. But the blockade of black uniforms was no match. Tank was the strongest guy on the Rebels. Quinn had watched in amazement as he bench-pressed 150 pounds in the weight room. Once Tank got up a head of steam, he was almost unstoppable.

Tank hit the Spartan wall and bounced right off like a rubber ball. But his legs kept thrusting and the wall kept moving backwards. Five . . . four . . . three . . . two . . . one. The yards of grass disappeared under him until there was only the goal line left. With three Spartans trying to block his path in front and two that had climbed onto his back, Tank plunged across the line with a final surge of power.

The referee blew his whistle and threw both hands high above his head to signal the touchdown.

"Touchdown!" Quinn shouted, pumping his fist into the air.

He ran into the end zone to help Tank get up from under the pile of Spartans. He was a lone red shirt under a stack of black jerseys. Soon the entire team was mobbing Tank. Braden, Carter, Jordan, and the rest of the players were high-fiving each other. They almost couldn't believe they had won. Sure, a convert still needed to be kicked through the goalposts to put them in the lead. But Jai Hundal was money in the bank when it came to booting single points. He had never missed before. He wasn't going to miss today. Final score: Rebels, 22–Spartans, 21.

Quinn and the Rebels whooped as they flew across the field back to the bench. All their aches and pains had magically disappeared. Quinn made a short stop to talk to his mom and dad, who had watched from the bleachers. They drove in from their home in the country for every game, rain or shine.

"Great game!" his dad said, patting Quinn on the shoulder pads.

"What a comeback!" His mom smiled, tugging the sleeve of his jersey.

Quinn heard footsteps running up behind him. "You were awesome!" Emma grabbed onto Quinn's other arm. "I wasn't sure you guys could do it!"

"A couple of lucky plays," Quinn kidded. "Any quarterback could have come off the bench in the second half and led the team to a touchdown on the last play of the game. It was nothing."

The Rebels thrust their scratched-up red helmets into the air as they filed into the gym's changing room. Carter went to his locker and pulled out his iPod. His playlist was famous throughout the school. He plugged the small silver unit into a pair of speakers and the room started groovin', rappin', and rockin' to Bruno Mars, Drake, and Pink.

Quinn thought this was going to be the Rebels' year. It was only the first win of the season but he and the rest of his teammates were in a partying mood. The only guy who didn't look happy was Luke Chambers. Quinn could understand why. Luke had started the game as the quarterback but Coach pulled him at halftime. He hadn't completed a single pass and the Rebels were held scoreless. But Quinn didn't feel sorry for him. *That's how football goes*, he thought. *You go with your best players and today I was the best*. Besides, Coach decided which quarterback would play, not Quinn.

Coach Gordon carried a chair into the middle of the noisy room and stood on it. He held out his arms, asking for quiet.

Quinn scanned the crowded locker room, trying to get his teammates' attention. The players were still celebrating. Jordan was bumping fists with Carter, while Tank and Braden were laughing it up with Jai.

Quinn's whistle pierced the air. "Coach has something to say!"

Coach pushed the brim of his Rebels cap up over his black hair. His brown eyes searched the faces in the room. "That was one heck of a game, guys." His voice cracked with emotion. "One of the best in the twenty years I've been coaching here at Riverbend."

"Rebels rock!" Tank shouted from the back.

"Every one of you deserves a game ball for your gritty performance out there this afternoon. I couldn't be more proud. But, as you know, the tradition is to award only one game ball to the most valuable player. Today, that player is . . . Quinn Brown."

The room exploded with cheers. "Quinn! Quinn! Quinn!" Everyone chanted except for Luke, who still sat scowling in the corner.

Coach Gordon flipped the pigskin to Quinn, who caught the pass and placed the ball into his locker. He'd keep it safe until it was given out to the MVP of the next game.

"Oh, and one more thing," Coach Gordon said as the room fell silent. "This was my last game as coach of the Rebels."

3 ORANGE CRUSH

"I sure didn't see that coming," Quinn said, sliding into the orange booth across from Emma. "Coach's announcement was a bombshell. The guys still can't believe it."

It was a Brown family tradition to eat at A&W after every game. Win or lose, Quinn always had a monster appetite.

"You guys rock this year," Emma said. "I hope Coach leaving isn't going to change that."

"Not as long as I'm playing," Quinn boasted.

"Very funny," Emma said. "You know it takes a whole team to win."

"Yeah, but it helps to have one good quarterback."

"You mean two good quarterbacks," she said, correcting him.

"Who, Luke? Yeah, whatever."

"The whole school is proud when the Rebels win," Emma said, beaming. "And I'm proud of you."

"We didn't show much pride last season. We sucked big time."

"Losing all those games wasn't your fault." Emma reached out her hand to cover Quinn's.

"Last year I was the only quarterback, so a lot of people blamed me for the losses. They said I wasn't in good enough shape. Or that I'd panic when the heat was on. What did they know?"

"They were just jealous of your being quarterback," Emma said, trying to make him feel better.

"Yeah, I made a few mistakes. But is that enough reason to make me share playing quarterback with Luke this year?"

"Coach must have thought it was the right decision," Emma said.

"I guess even he can make a mistake."

Quinn's mom squeezed into the booth and his dad stood beside her.

Quinn glanced at his dad. Every time Quinn saw him he seemed to be a little bit shorter and a little bit paunchier around the middle. Or maybe it was just that Quinn was still growing and was now the same height. He had to admit that he secretly liked looking his dad in the eye.

"Pull up a chair, Shorty." Quinn laughed.

"Good thing you're a better quarterback than comedian," his dad said, grinning. "Now, who's hungry?"

"Not too many fries, Sam. You know what the doctor said about your health." Quinn's mom worried his dad was eating too much fast food and getting fat. She had seen too many patients suffering from heart disease at the hospital where she worked as a nurse in the emergency room.

"Yeah, yeah, yeah," his dad said. "So, how about if I go get the food? Emma, what would you like?"

"She'll have the usual," Quinn interrupted before Emma could reply.

Emma narrowed her eyes. "How do you know what I want? Maybe I don't want my usual?"

"All right! All right!" Quinn said, backing off.

Moments later, his dad returned, carrying a tray overflowing with burgers, nuggets, fries, and big cups of Coke.

"Give your father a hand," his mom said.

"But I just sat down," Quinn complained.

Emma jumped up. "I can help him, Mrs. Brown."

Quinn shot Emma a disapproving look. *She was always being nice. Sometimes a little too nice*, Quinn thought.

Four eager hands reached in to grab the food as Quinn's mom asked the question on everyone's mind. "Why do you think Coach is leaving?"

Quinn's dad put down his Papa Burger. "You know, he's been running the team for a long time. Maybe he's had enough and wants to hang up his coaching whistle for good."

"But after the first game of the season?" Quinn said, shaking his head. "It doesn't make sense."

"Especially since you won," his mom chipped in.

"Maybe he wants to go back to just being a teacher," Emma said. "I have him for second period social studies and he's fantastic. He really knows his history, especially the wars."

Quinn nodded. "That's why he's such an awesome coach. He knows how to march into enemy territory and capture six points. It's a war out there on the field and he's like Napoleon."

"Except taller." Emma laughed.

Quinn watched the front door of the restaurant swing open. Luke and his cheerleader girlfriend, Prita, strolled in like they owned the place. Luke swaggered past the tables, fist-bumping some of the other Rebels who had also stopped by for a victory meal. Quinn did a slow burn. Why would he be pounding fists with the other players when he got pulled in the first half?

"I could have led the team to that touchdown, too," Luke bragged to a couple of players wearing red Rebels jackets. "Coach just needed to put me back in the game."

Luke and Prita moved through the aisles like a king and queen. They smiled and waved at everyone they passed. With their flowing hair and bright teeth, the only things missing were their capes and glittery crowns.

After they ordered their burgers at the counter, Quinn watched the royal couple scan the restaurant for a place to sit. He could almost see them plotting their next move. They could have sat far away, but instead they chose a booth just close enough for someone to hear every word if he wanted to. And Quinn did.

"I can't wait for the new coach to see me play," Luke boasted.

"You'll impress him," Prita said. "You should play quarterback way more than Quinn."

"I know. Once the new coach sees me throw the ball, he'll never take me out."

Quinn rolled his eyes at Emma. "Are you listening to that crap?"

"What crap?" Emma whispered. "The only people I'm listening to are your parents."

"Luke and Prita are dissing us three tables away."

Emma shrugged. "You shouldn't care so much what other people think of you."

Quinn ignored Emma and turned to eavesdrop some more.

"You're just what the team needs," Prita gushed.

"I think another team needs a change, too," Luke said.

"What do you mean?"

"I'm talking about the cheerleading team," Luke said.

"Totally."

"Emma doesn't know the routines nearly as well as you."

Prita shook her head. "How she ever got to be head cheerleader, I'll never know."

Quinn didn't want to hear another word. Luke wasn't half the quarterback he was. And Prita wasn't nearly as good a cheerleader as Emma. "I think I've lost my appetite," Quinn announced to the table. "Let's bounce."

"I'm still working on my second burger," his dad said, looking surprised at Quinn's sudden change of plans.

"Why the rush, son?" his mom asked. "We're still enjoying our meals."

"Then you stay here. Emma and I are splitting, right Em?"

Quinn stood to leave as Emma scowled at him.

"I guess you've decided for me."

4 SLICK

Quinn pulled his red jersey over his shoulder pads, picked up his helmet, and headed out of the locker room. His whole body still ached from all the hits he had taken from the gigantic Spartans defensive line. He jogged onto the field and joined Luke, Carter, Jordan, and the rest of the team. The players had formed a large half-circle in front of Coach Gordon. It was a crisp September afternoon and the sky was as blue as an Indianapolis Colts uniform. Coach wore his usual Rebels hoodie like it was just another practice. But this day would prove to be anything but ordinary.

Coach stretched out his arm and pointed to the grey door the players had just come from. "Every time you walk through that door, it's an opportunity. A chance to prove yourself in the next practice, the next game, the next challenge."

Quinn watched Coach's eyes move from player to player. "My 'door' was a job offer to become president of the Calgary High School Football League. I get to run the league and choose the players for the all-star team that plays in the Canadian Championship."

Coach's decision to leave made more sense to Quinn now. Becoming the head honcho of the league was a big deal. And coaching the all-star team was a real honour. Making that team had always been a dream for Quinn.

"Managing the whole league is going to be a big challenge, but I want to give it my best shot. The same way I want you all to give it your best shot for the new coach. That means I want Quinn, Luke, and everyone else standing here to do what he says. He was the quarterback on that all-star team when he played for me here at Riverbend twenty years ago. I know he's going to be an awesome coach, starting today."

Quinn had heard about a legendary quarterback from years ago. He had seen old photographs of a QB throwing passes in the awards showcase along the hall outside the gym. Everyone knew Mike "the Rifle" Miller still held the school record for most touchdowns thrown in a single season.

Suddenly, a hulking figure pushed open the door and walked briskly across the field.

Coach smiled as he reached out and shook the man's hand. "I want you all to welcome Coach Miller."

The new coach was thick as a tree trunk and must have stood at least six foot four. He was the strongest, tallest guy on the field. Quinn saw that he was a lot slicker than Coach Gordon, too. Instead of a red hoodie, he wore a grey suit. Instead of black cleats, he wore shiny, black leather shoes. Instead of an old Rebels hat, he wore his hair short with a trim beard to match.

Coach Gordon waved one last goodbye to the team. "Thanks for everything, guys. I'm leaving with a lot of great memories. Maybe I'll see some of you on the all-star team at the end of the season." Then he turned and headed across the grass towards the school.

A few of the players started to clap their hands and chant: "Coach! . . . Coach!" It didn't take long before the whole team was cheering as one. "Coach! Coach! Coach!" The chants grew until he reached the corner of the school and disappeared out of sight.

At five foot ten, Quinn thought he was tall, but Coach Miller towered over him and the rest of the Rebels. He was a man standing next to boys.

"You may be wondering why I'm all dressed up like this." Coach Miller pointed two big thumbs back at the lapels of his expensive suit. "It's because coaching isn't my only job. I'm also in the stockbroking business and I came here straight from my office. I intend to run this team like a business, too."

Quinn didn't know what to make of the brash new coach. He clearly wasn't laid-back like Coach Gordon. Quinn knew he'd better pay attention, though. He didn't want to get fired from his quarterback position on Coach Miller's first day.

"If you're doing your job and your stock is going up, you'll play," Coach Miller explained. "If you're not performing and your stock is going down, you won't. It's that simple. I know Coach Gordon had his favourite players. But that doesn't wash with me. This is a whole new ball game. From now on each one of you will have to prove yourself to me."

Quinn's heart started to race again. The new coach wasn't going to help him like the old coach. His eyes darted away from Coach Miller and he caught Luke staring at him with a cold smile. This was Luke's chance and Quinn knew he'd do almost anything to impress the new coach. Quinn had to stay on guard.

Coach Miller pulled a black whistle out of his suit pocket and hung the cord around his neck. He blew one short burst. "Quarterbacks and receivers come with me. Everyone else get ready to practise their hitting against the padded sleds." He pointed to the heavy equipment that had to be pushed along the ground by four players at a time.

Quinn kept his distance from Luke as he followed Coach Miller, Carter, Jordan, and a handful of receivers to the middle of the field.

"Let's do some quick pass patterns," Coach said, grabbing a football in his big right hand. "These will be our bread-and-butter plays and I want you guys to be able to run them in your sleep." He tossed the ball to Quinn. "Brown, show me what you've got."

Quinn eyed the Rebels' speediest receiver. "Carter, let's start with a simple pattern. A ten-yard square out to the left sideline."

Quinn held the ball out in front of him, pretending to take the snap. "Ready . . . set . . . hut!" He backpedalled a few yards, gripping the pigskin tightly in his right hand. Carter took off from the line, ran straight for ten yards, then cut to his left, gunning for the sideline. Quinn pulled his arm back and fired. The ball wobbled like a wounded duck as it flew just behind Carter, landing harmlessly on the grass.

Coach Miller narrowed his eyes. "What was that, Brown? This isn't peewee football. It's a good thing this is just a practice. We can't have that happening next game, against the Cowboys."

Quinn hung his head. This never happened. He knew he had to throw the ball in front of Carter so he could keep running. Throwing behind the receiver was a rookie mistake. Quinn wondered what had gotten into him. Was he freezing up because the old coach was leaving? Or because the new coach was arriving? Whatever it was, he'd better get it together fast.

"Chambers, you're up," Coach Miller said. He took the ball from Quinn and flipped it to his competition. Luke called the signals and Jordan sprinted from the line, turning left at ten yards. He threw a perfect short pass just in front of the receiver, who easily caught the ball then jogged back to where Coach Miller was standing.

"Nice work, Chambers," Coach Miller said, smiling. "Looks to me like you're going to give Brown a run for his money. I'd say your quarterback stock is definitely going up."

5 PARABOLA

Quinn stood alone at his locker. The hall was completely empty. All the other kids were on their way to class, just like he should have been. It wasn't as if he had a good reason for still being there. He wasn't talking to anyone. He wasn't fumbling around looking for his books or checking his phone for a text from Emma. He was just ... killing time. For the next forty minutes his mission was to survive math class. Finally, just before the bell sounded, he pulled out his books and rushed down the hall.

Even as he approached the classroom his heart started to race. It was the same feeling of panic he had in some games. He'd always worry about making a mistake. In football, it was throwing a bad pass. In math class, it was giving the wrong answer. On the field, he fretted that Coach and the players might think he wasn't good enough — the same way his math teacher and the other kids might think he wasn't smart enough. His stomach was in knots.

Quinn took a deep breath and slipped into the

classroom just as Mrs. Devlin was closing the door. "Nice of you to join us, Mr. Brown," she said, squinting her hawk-like eyes.

He took his usual spot at the back with a handful of other players from the team. He hoped his teammates could protect him from the teacher, the same way they guarded him during the games. Carter and Jordan sat just ahead, wearing their red Rebels jackets. Luke and Braden took up their positions two rows over, trash-talking as usual.

"Let's get this class in gear," Luke said loudly enough for the whole class to hear. "Practice starts in an hour and I've got some sweet passes to throw."

Mrs. Devlin walked down the aisle, her heels clicking on the hard tile floor. Quinn's palms started to sweat. He could almost hear her asking him a question — a question he wouldn't know the answer to. Then, by some stroke of luck, the teacher stopped beside Luke. Her neck twisted and her tiny eyes shifted their gaze from Quinn to Luke.

"Mr. Chambers, let's talk about those sweet passes you make."

"They're perfect spirals, every one," Luke said.

Quinn bit his lip. Luke couldn't throw a decent spiral if his life depended on it.

Mrs. Devlin gave Luke a thin smile, not quite believing him. "Yes, I'm sure they are. Now, why don't you describe for me what mathematical path the ball takes when you throw that perfect pass?"

"The path right to the receiver," Luke joked. "Probably for a touchdown."

When the laughter in the class died down, Mrs. Devlin continued her questioning. "I'm going to give you one last chance to reply before I assume you haven't done your homework."

Luke's mouth stayed shut tight.

"I thought so," Mrs. Devlin said, shaking her head. "Anyone else care to answer this question?"

Quinn ducked under his desk and pretended to tie his shoelace. He didn't have a clue what the answer was, even though his passes were a lot better than Luke's.

Suddenly a hand shot up at the front of the classroom. Quinn glanced up from the floor but didn't recognize the black-haired boy. *Must be new,* he thought. The boy seemed like any other Riverbend student — hoodie, jeans, and a pair of extra-sturdy hiking shoes. From the look of his muscular arms he might even play sports. But something about him was different. Quinn didn't know exactly what.

Mrs. Devlin turned away from Luke, who continued to clown around. She walked back to the blackboard, passing the new student, who still had his arm raised in the air.

"Hold that response, Walker."

The teacher picked up a piece of chalk and drew a long white curve from one end of the board to the other. "Say this line was the flight of Luke's perfect football pass. The shape of that curved line would be called a . . ."

"Parabola," Walker said.

"A *p-a-r-a-b-o-l-a*," Mrs. Devlin said to the class, slowly pronouncing every letter. "Very good, Walker."

"I'll remember to throw a *p-a-r-a-b-o-l-a* next time I pass," Luke said, glaring at the new guy.

After another half-hour of dodging questions, Quinn made his escape. He wasn't the first to leave the classroom. Luke and his buddy Braden bolted for the door the second the bell rang. Braden was the team's centre and a lot stockier than Quinn. He acted like Luke's bodyguard and led the way out of the classroom.

Despite everyone rushing for the exit, Walker remained seated at his desk. Quinn thought the new kid must be trying to impress Mrs. Devlin by getting a jump on his homework. Something only a nerd would do.

A few minutes later Quinn pulled up at his locker, thumbed his combination, and pulled open the door. Just a few feet away, Luke and Braden were getting ready to head down to the gym to suit up for practice.

"What kind of name is Walker, anyway?" Luke asked. "Pretty wimpy, if you ask me."

Braden nodded. "He's got a lot of nerve making a quarterback like you look bad in class. He's going to have to learn his place."

There was a loud *click* down the hall.

Quinn turned to see the door to his math classroom slowly swing open. He thought everyone had left a long time ago. But now someone was hobbling through the doorway.

The boy walked awkwardly, with a heavy limp. It was like he had a broken foot, but Quinn saw no cast. He wore a hoodie and shuffled in the other direction. Quinn wasn't the only one who witnessed the boy slipping out of the classroom.

"Now, what do we have here?" Luke said, starting to walk down the hall toward the boy. "Hey, Gimpy!" The boy continued to limp away, doing his best to go faster. "Hey, I'm talking to you!"

The chase was on but it wasn't even close. Quinn watched Luke and Braden quickly catch up to the boy. He gave up, stopped, and turned to meet the two bigger and faster football players who had tracked him down. Now that Quinn could see the boy's black hair and face, he knew for sure it was the new kid from his math class — Walker.

Quinn stayed at his locker but he could hear every word echo down the hall.

"Not so fast, Peg Leg," Luke said.

Braden joined in. "Don't worry, Luke, it doesn't look like he could go fast even if he wanted to." Both guys laughed.

Walker stood silently taking the taunts, staring right back at Luke and Braden with steely eyes.

"What's your name?" Luke asked.

"Walker Woods," he replied.

"You're joking, right?" Braden snorted.

"My name isn't a joke."

"'Walker' sure seems like a funny name for a guy who can barely walk," Luke said, staring down at the boy's leg.

"I can walk fine," Walker said.

"Well, you better get walking," Luke said. "This is the hall where the football team hangs out. Why don't you go find your locker, wherever that is? Maybe in the cripple hall."

Braden looked up at the hallway clock. "Let's bail, Luke. Practice starts in fifteen minutes."

Luke and Braden were still laughing as they rushed past Quinn on their way to the locker room. Quinn cast one last glance at the boy with black hair shuffling down the empty hallway. After a moment, he looked the other way as if nothing had happened and followed his teammates down to the gym.

6 PLAYING SHORT

Only two more laps to go. That was what Quinn kept saying to himself as he dragged his tired body around the edge of the football field.

At the end of practice, Coach Miller had ordered the whole team to run ten laps. If Quinn thought that was tough on him, all he had to do was look behind to see the big, heavy linemen struggling with every pounding step. Even Tank, the sturdy fullback, was feeling the pain. Quinn saw him stop to take a long swig from his water bottle. He wondered whether Tank was really thirsty or just needed a break for his worn-out legs.

This was no jog in the park. When you're a football player, you don't just wear a T-shirt, shorts, and running shoes like the cross-country team. You have to strap on your heavy helmet, shoulder pads, pants, and cleats. Sure, the equipment keeps you from getting hurt, but you have to lug it everywhere you run. And for Quinn and his teammates, right now that was ten times around the Riverbend field on a scorching Tuesday afternoon.

Just one more lap.

"Okay, let's bring it in," Coach Miller said, clapping his hands. The dark, grey business suit was gone but he was still dressed for work in a brown jacket and tie. Quinn wondered how many clothes Coach had in his closet. Probably a ton more than he did. Quinn's entire wardrobe was three pairs of pants, six T-shirts, and one dress shirt for special occasions, like Thanksgiving dinner at his grandparents'. He had a bunch of hoodies too, for when the weather got cooler.

Quinn joined the pack of players who were limping and groaning their way to where Coach Miller stood on the sideline. With Coach Gordon, Quinn never had to train much, which was just the way he liked it. He was a quarterback, after all. All he had to do was make hand-offs and pass the ball. He didn't think he had to be in good shape like the other guys. Until today, that is. Today he was beat just like everyone else.

"I want to tell you why I ordered laps at the end of practice today," Coach said. "I didn't do it to be mean or make you suffer. I had a good reason."

Quinn looked over at Luke, who was hanging his head and panting. At least he wasn't the only dog-tired quarterback.

"When I studied the roster for this year's team I noticed one important fact — we don't have enough players."

"You know it, Coach," Carter complained.

Quinn nodded in agreement with the rest of the players.

"It makes sense," Coach explained. "Riverbend Junior High is a small school. We don't have a big number of students like Sprucewood. They can choose from a hundred players. We can pick from only thirty. That's just not enough. That's why other teams come back against us in the fourth quarter and sometimes we end up losing. We're just too tired."

"You're not kidding," Tank said, still breathing hard.

"So, I have a two-point plan to fix that," Coach continued. "First, we're going to be the most fit team in the league. That means everyone, including the quarterbacks." He stared at Quinn and Luke. "And second, we're going to look for more players. Guys who might not have played football before but who want to give it a try and help their school. Guys who want to proudly wear Rebels red."

Quinn wasn't so sure that was a good idea. *Wouldn't guys who wanted to play football already be playing football?* The only dudes left were slackers who couldn't catch or throw a ball if their lives depended on it. This could turn into a gong show.

Coach wasn't finished. "We still have another half-hour of practice before we hit the showers. We're going to split up into two teams to see how our offence plays against our defence. But first, let's hit the ground and do fifty sit-ups and fifty push-ups."

Groans spread though the team like a wave.

Quinn and his teammates dropped to the turf and gave Coach fifty. He didn't like having to do the same amount of work as everyone else. He collapsed on his face after his last push-up, but there was no time to rest. Coach was barking out more orders.

"Okay, I want the offence to start at midfield and run a series of plays to get into the end zone. Defence, pretend it's the fourth quarter. Even though you're tired, you have to keep them from scoring to win the game. Brown, you start at QB."

The twelve offensive players put on their helmets and trotted onto the field to huddle. Quinn stood in the middle of his teammates and called a square-out to Jordan — the same simple pass play they had run at the previous practice.

Quinn grabbed the snap from Braden and stepped back into the pocket. His five beefy offensive linemen protected him from the defensive rush so he had time to throw the ball. He watched Jordan bolt from the line of scrimmage, run straight, then square out to his left.

Quinn passed the ball to where he thought Jordan would be, but he was way off. Unlike last time when he threw behind the receiver, this time he tossed the ball way out front. Not even Jordan could run fast enough to catch this wobbly pass. The pigskin thudded to the ground and skidded along the grass.

"Incomplete!" Coach shouted from the sideline. "It's second down, Brown. You've got one more chance."

Quinn couldn't believe he had thrown another bad pass. He was sucking big time. But he was determined to complete a pass and show the new coach why he was a better quarterback than Luke.

For the next play he called a square-out to the right, this time for Carter. Braden snapped the ball again and Quinn backpedalled into the pocket. He spotted Carter streaking to the right sideline and fired a perfect spiral. A perfectly thrown pass . . . that sailed ten feet over Carter's head!

Carter shot a look back at Quinn and shook his head. "What was that, man?"

Coach cupped his hands and shouted out another order. "Chambers, go in for Brown! Let's get the team moving. Show me what you've got."

"Move aside, Brown," Luke jeered. "Watch how a real pro does it."

Quinn got the message loud and clear. He wasn't getting the job done and he knew it. Maybe he was out of shape. Maybe he was getting rattled. But one thing was for sure — he didn't want Luke to take over playing quarterback. That would be the worst.

Coach waved in Quinn from the huddle. He started to jog toward the sideline and saw Luke coming toward him with a big smile on his face. *What a jerk*, he thought. Luke was running straight at him. Quinn wasn't about to back down. If anyone was going to get out of the way it was going to be Luke. He was probably just bluffing, anyway. The players were like two runaway freight trains racing at each other on the same track.

Smash!

Luke slammed into Quinn's shoulder as he ran past, sending him sprawling to the turf.

Quinn lay dazed on the ground. He burned inside, embarrassed by how this must look to Coach and his team. He got up on one knee and took a deep breath to steady himself. Then he slowly stood up and walked woozily to the sideline. Quinn's shoulder was bruised but not as much as his pride. Luke had made it look like an accident. But it was no accident at all.

7 BAD TO WORSE

Mrs. Devlin stood at the front of the class. She clutched a stack of white papers in her bony claws. "I've marked your tests from last week and the results are pretty clear. Some of you need extra help."

Quinn gulped. This couldn't be good news. He knew he wasn't another Einstein. Still, he always did his homework and had no problem with social science or any other subject. But math was another story. Every time he sat down for a test he'd go into panic mode. It was like pulling a fire alarm in his brain. He couldn't even answer the questions he had studied the night before.

The birdlike teacher flitted around the class, dropping off tests on desks. She gave each student a look as she passed by. A smile that said "keep up the good work" to kids who did well. And a thin-lipped frown to kids who didn't make the grade.

Mrs. Devlin hovered over Quinn's desk like a hummingbird. "You can do better." Quinn picked up the paper and turned it over to reveal the mark. There it was, up in the right-hand corner. A big "50%" scrawled in bright red ink. It was one of the worst marks he had ever gotten, but at least he had passed. If he hadn't, there would have been big trouble at home. His parents had made it clear that to keep playing football, he had to get good marks.

"Work hard every day, or you don't play," his dad always said.

A couple of rows away Luke was bragging. "Seventy-five per cent — all right! This was too easy." He shot a glance over at Quinn. "If you're not smart enough to ace this test, maybe you're not smart enough to play quarterback, either."

Quinn narrowed his eyes and squeezed his pencil so hard he thought it might snap in half. He couldn't believe Luke's mark. He didn't even know what a parabola was! How could he have rocked the exam?

Mrs. Devlin winged her way to the front of the class. "Starting today, I'm organizing an after-school help program. It's called Tutor Time. You don't have to sign up but I'd recommend that you do if you want better grades."

Quinn looked up from his paper and saw the teacher's beady eyes looking right at him.

"I'll be matching students who had trouble with students who did really well."

Quinn buried his head in his textbook. He didn't want help. All he needed was a little more time to figure things out himself. And he sure didn't want anyone else thinking he needed help, especially Luke.

"By the way," Mrs. Devlin said, moving beside the new student's desk, "Walker was the only one to get a perfect mark on his test." The teacher patted the new kid's shoulder.

The bell rang and Quinn shoved the test in his math binder. He couldn't get out of class fast enough. He thought he had made his escape but halfway to the door he heard a familiar screech. "Quinn, can you please stay after class for a few minutes?"

He froze.

"Why don't you come sit here, next to Walker," Mrs. Devlin said. "I have a wonderful idea for both of you."

Wonderful? Bad, terrible, awful, and crappy might have been better words, he thought. Quinn knew what was coming next. He slunk back to the seat beside Walker but couldn't look him in the eye.

"I thought you and Walker would be a perfect match for Tutor Time," Mrs. Devlin said, smiling. "Walker is a brilliant student, and Quinn, well, you're filled with potential. Plus, this would be a good way for Walker to get to know someone in the class. It's not easy when you're new."

"I'm game," Walker said. He looked embarrassed by the teacher's compliment.

Quinn had to think fast. "I don't know, Mrs. Devlin.

I have a pretty busy schedule with football and every-thing. I'm not sure I'd have time."

"Doesn't the football team require good grades for you to keep playing?"

"Yes, but I'm sure my next test will be better."

Mrs. Devlin looked skeptical. "Well, if it's not, you know where to find Walker," she said, tapping the desk.

But Quinn was already headed for the door. And he wasn't looking back.

***

It was feeding time at "the zoo." All the animals were gobbling down sandwiches while sharing the latest school gossip in high-pitched squeals. Emma waved from a small table in the corner of the noisy cafeteria. Her eyes tracked Quinn as he snaked through the crowded tables to her side.

She didn't look happy. Her smile was gone. Her hands were clasped together on her lap. And her lips stayed tightly shut until she spoke.

"I've been waiting for you."

"Sorry I'm late, but I got hung up in math class," Quinn said.

"How did your test go?" she asked.

"Freakin' awful. Getting a low mark was bad enough, but now it's even worse."

"What happened?"

Quinn shifted uneasily in his chair. "Devlin kept me after class and said I should get tutored by that new gimpy kid, Walker."

"Why did you call him gimpy?" Emma asked, her voice starting to rise.

"Because he is. He's got only one good leg. The other one is all twisted up or something."

Emma's eyes narrowed. "That's pretty harsh, Quinn. He's just a new kid trying to fit in. And he happens to have a bad leg. You calling him a gimp doesn't help."

"That's nothing," Quinn said, locking eyes with her. "You should have heard what Luke called him."

"I did hear." Emma leaned forward. "It was horrible. No one deserves to be called that. I also heard you saw it all and did nothing."

Quinn's eyes grew wide. "What could I do?"

"Lots! You could have gone over there and stopped Luke. You could have stood up for the new kid."

"Why would I do that?" Quinn said, throwing up his hands.

Emma was furious now. "Because he can't stand up for himself!"

"How would you know?"

"I know plenty!" Emma snapped. "Remember, I volunteer at the children's hospital. I see kids who can't walk properly all the time. They have a hard enough time without putting up with bullies calling them names."

Quinn furrowed his brow. "I thought you would take my side. See things my way."

"I'm sick of being expected to see things your way," Emma snarled. Her face was flushed with anger. "The only person you think of is you, you, you! You don't think the other players on the team matter. You don't think you have to help your father. You don't even care what *I* think. And you certainly don't think kids like Walker need help."

Emma pushed herself away from the table and stood up.

"Hey, where are you going?" Quinn blurted.

"If you don't care about others, then I'm not sure I can care about you."

"W-what do you mean?" Quinn asked, searching her face.

Emma said only three words before disappearing into the streaming maze of kids.

"We're breaking up."

8 THE TRYOUT

The poster was tacked to the bulletin board just inside the main entrance of the school. The words were so big that Quinn could read them as soon as he walked through the front doors.

PLAYERS WANTED!

The Rebels football team needs you.
If you can pass, block, tackle, kick, run, or even walk, you're invited to try out. The next practice is today at 4:00 sharp. Be there.

GO, REBELS!

Quinn shook his head. *This is crazy.* Just because you put on a helmet and a pair of cleats doesn't mean you're a football player. You have to want it. Have to dream about it. Have to have natural talent like he had. Hard work could get you only so far. He could just imagine what kind of guys were going to show up at the tryout after school. It was going to be a circus.

Quinn shuffled through his day. His brain was thick with confusion. Yeah, he was struggling with math but did that mean he had to be tutored by some new kid in the class?

No way. So what if that guy got 100% on his test? He was a math geek. Of course, it wasn't totally Walker's fault. Mrs. Devlin had roped him into it. But he didn't have to go along. He could have said he didn't want to help the school quarterback. He could have said he didn't want to make new friends.

He sat through his classes like a zombie from *The Walking Dead*. He was just lucky none of his teachers asked him any questions. All he could think about was Emma. How could she be his girlfriend one minute and then not the next? He had never seen her so upset. Quinn wondered if what she said was true. Did he only think of himself? Did he care about the other players on the team? Or his dad? Or even Emma? And what about Walker? Did it matter that Luke had picked on him?

By the time four o'clock rolled around, Quinn was glad the school day was over and he could escape to practice. For the next ninety minutes he could focus on something other than math problems and Emma problems. He dashed down to the locker room, put on his uniform, and headed for the field.

Dressed in a grey suit, Coach Miller stood at the fifty-yard line waiting to see how many players his recruitment poster had attracted. It must have been a success. Coach was already talking to a circle of guys Quinn had never seen at practice before.

To Quinn they were a group of lame misfits. There were body shapes of every size. From watermelon boy, who looked so round he must have rolled onto the field, all the way to stick boy, who was so skinny a puff of wind could have knocked him over. Quinn knew they needed more players but was this gang of cartoon characters going to get them to the championship? *Get real*.

It didn't seem to bother Coach, though. "Welcome, men, and thanks for coming out." He gave the six new guys a rare smile. "As you know, we've got a few positions to fill. Most of them are to back up our first-string players. Go in for them when they get injured or tired late in the game. The roles you fill may not seem important, but make no mistake — they're crucial to helping the Rebels win games."

Coach took a couple of steps back and surveyed the jumble of new recruits. "Now, if there are no more new players, we'll get the practice underway and see what you guys have got."

"Coach, someone else is walking over," Luke said with a laugh. "Or at least *trying* to walk over."

Quinn turned with the rest of the team to watch.

He couldn't believe what he saw.

Hobbling across the grass was Walker, wearing red sweatpants and a white T-shirt. He limped along one step at a time until he stood with the rest of the rookies in front of Coach. Every player stared.

"You must have the wrong tryout," Luke said. "This isn't the glee club or some kind of charity bingo. This is the football team, dude."

Coach held up his hand. "That's enough, Chambers. What's your name, son?"

"Woods, sir."

"It took a lot of guts for you to come out here, Woods. In business, attitude counts for a lot. I'm impressed by that. But I have to say I'm not sure what position you can play. You don't seem to be able to block or tackle or even run."

Walker nodded. "You're right, sir. I can't do any of those things. But the poster also said *walk*, and I can do that. I could hold the ball when field goals and converts are kicked."

Coach studied Walker up and down, from the awkward way he stood to the determined look on his face. "At my company I'll always give someone a chance, but then it's up to them to prove themselves," Coach said. "Grab a helmet, Woods. You're on the team."

As soon as Coach stepped away to talk to another group of players, Luke moved in like a jackal.

"I'm watching you, man," he said, spitting his words

in Walker's face. "If you ever drop the ball on a field goal, I'll complain to Coach. If we ever miss an extra point because of you, I'll complain to Coach. I'll be your worst nightmare if you screw up even once."

Quinn didn't know what to do. Emma would have told him to step in, but he couldn't. He knew he shouldn't agree with Luke or question Coach's decision to let Walker play. But he couldn't see how a guy with just one good leg could help the team.

9 PRESS

Quinn watched her across the crowded cafeteria. She was sitting and laughing with two other cheerleaders at a table in the corner — their corner. He wondered how Emma could be in such a good mood. He sure wasn't. He was tired from not sleeping well. He'd tossed and turned all night, his head filled with nightmares of Emma slamming doors in his face and never wanting to see him again. And he was hungry from not eating his regular triple-decker sandwiches, thanks to the knot in his stomach. He hated splitting up.

Another math class had just ended. Another class where Mrs. Devlin had given back another quiz with another low mark. She had even written a note at the top of the page: "Time for a tutor?"

It sure wasn't the mark he was hoping for. If his grades didn't start improving fast he might get kicked off the team. And it wasn't just his parents who needed him to do well. There was also a school rule that every player had to get over 65% in every class to keep playing. He had a long way to go to get that in math.

Quinn watched the three girls finish their lunch and walk to the exit. Maybe if Emma just saw him. Maybe she would instantly want to get back together. Maybe if he just happened to bump into her by accident. That would do it.

Quinn jumped up from his chair and sprinted to the exit like he was running for a first down. He had to make sure he beat Emma there. He flew into the hallway and spun around, doing a one-eighty. Then he started walking back into the cafeteria like he hadn't been there before.

"Hey, Em, what a surprise to see you here!"

Emma's eyes locked on Quinn and grew wide with surprise. That was just the reaction he'd hoped for. He was sure this "chance meeting" was all she needed to fall for him all over again. Quinn opened his arms, ready for Emma to hug him. But instead of wrapping her arms around him, she linked arms with her two friends and ran down the hall.

Quinn stood frozen while kids sped by on their way to class. His mind raced. This hadn't gone down like he'd planned. Emma wasn't spending every minute of the day thinking about him. She wasn't thinking about him at all.

Then things went from bad to worse. Prita and Luke came snickering down the hallway.

"What's the matter, Quinn?" Prita asked. "Did the evil witch turn you into a statue?"

"Hope she didn't cast a spell on your quarterback skills." Luke laughed. "A couple more bad passes and you might turn into a pumpkin."

Quinn's face turned Rebels red. He was angry, confused, and embarrassed all at the same time. It seemed everyone was against him. He needed to blow off steam. There was no practice after school today. Coach said he had a big business meeting that afternoon and couldn't make it. Quinn planned to go to the weight room instead. He hoped working out would let him chill and forget about what just happened with Emma, Prita, and Luke.

The final bell rang and Quinn headed down the stairs. The weight room had a glass wall that looked out into the big gym. Inside it was filled with treadmills, exercise bikes, barbells, and different weight machines. There was always a teacher there to make sure you were using the equipment safely after school or at lunch. If you were a football, basketball, hockey, volleyball, or soccer player, it was where you'd go to get stronger.

Quinn opened the door and scanned the room. He didn't expect any other players to be there. Everyone else on the team would be glad to have the day off. Their bodies were still beat up and tired after the tough practices Coach had been putting them through. He wanted to make sure they were ready for the next game against Rockport.

From a distance he saw a teacher helping someone pump iron at the bench press. Quinn could see only the red sweatpants that covered the athlete's legs. The top part of his body was out of view, blocked by the machine. As Quinn got closer he could see how much weight the guy's arms were pressing up over his head. *That must be over two hundred pounds!* No one on the team could bench-press that much, not even Tank. It must've been one of the other big gym teachers staying in shape.

Quinn crept around the corner, not wanting to interrupt the teacher's workout. One look and he stopped dead in his tracks. The guy pressing the big stack of steel weights was no teacher.

Quinn gasped. "Walker! What are you doing here?"

The biceps of the new boy bulged as he finished pushing up the bar for the last time. The teacher made sure the weight was safely in place and went to the water fountain. Walker let out a long breath and sat up on the bench. "I want to make sure I'm strong enough to be the best ball-holder I can be. So I'm just doing some small arm presses to get in shape."

"Small?" Quinn said, his eyes widening. "Are you kidding me? I've never seen anyone push that kind of weight."

Walker shrugged. "Then I guess the other players don't push themselves hard enough."

Quinn wondered if he had misjudged Walker. Maybe Emma was right. Maybe he wasn't just a math-nerd.

He may have a problem with his leg but he was doing everything in his power to make up for it by having a super-strong upper body. That took a lot of effort. A lot more effort than Quinn was giving to his training or his math.

"Hey, Walker, I've been thinking about that math tutoring program Mrs. Devlin was talking about."

"It's okay, man. I understand if you don't want my help."

"No, it's just the opposite. I do want your help."

Walker smiled. "Really?"

"Yeah, I just can't do it at school. I don't have time since we have football practice every day after class."

"What about on the weekend?" Walker asked.

Quinn thought for a minute. "Sure, why don't you come over to my house on Sunday? I'll email you the directions."

"I'll be there," Walker said. "Here. Spot for me." Then he slid under the impossibly heavy pile of weights and pushed up one more time.

10 THE TIRE

"What time is your math tutor getting here?" Quinn's mom asked. She stood at the kitchen sink gazing out the window at the long, tree-lined driveway. Quinn lived in a large white farmhouse on a sprawling acreage. His house was only a short distance from the edge of the city limits, but it seemed way out in the country. There was a view of the snow-capped Rocky Mountains, and the blue sky seemed to go on forever.

"Two o'clock, any minute," Quinn said, tying up his running shoes.

The property was no longer a working farm. There were no chickens or pigs or cows. But there was a large garden in the backyard where they grew corn, carrots, lettuce, peas, beans, and a few other vegetables. Quinn's mom thought it was important to serve fresh produce at every meal. It was all part of her "keeping healthy" thing, since she was a nurse.

Quinn stepped out the front door to wait for Walker. The yard smelled of freshly cut grass. He was the regular lawn mower now that his dad complained of being "done in" every time he tackled the weekly chore. Quinn could understand why it tired him out. The yard was as big as a football field.

Quinn picked up an old, weathered football lying on the ground. He pretended he was in a game. He looked downfield and spotted his receiver — a black tire tied to a rope hanging from a tall poplar tree. Quinn took a few steps back, pointed his shoulder at the target, cocked his arm, and fired. The pigskin sailed thirty yards through the air, hitting the rubber of the tire. It wasn't a bull's eye through the hole but if it had been a real pass, Carter or Jordan would have easily caught it. Those guys had hands like glue.

Quinn nodded to himself. *Yeah.*

A small blue car drove down the gravel driveway, rolling to a stop by the farmhouse. The passenger door opened and Walker eased himself out. He waved to the driver as the car headed back down the driveway.

"Hey, man, thanks for coming," Quinn said, smiling.

"No problem." Walker shrugged. "When are we going to get started? I've got our textbook and some old tests in my backpack that we can go over."

"Right after I throw a few passes," Quinn said. "Got to keep the arm in shape."

Walker pointed at the swinging tire. "That looks like a tough target."

"Almost impossible to hit the bull's-eye."

"Mind if I try?"

Quinn tossed the football to Walker. "Be my guest, but don't say I didn't warn you."

Walker grabbed the pigskin in his strong right hand and started hobbling the other way. "Let's make this interesting."

"You're going the wrong way, dude. The tire is way down at the other end of the yard."

"I know."

Quinn watched Walker pace another twenty yards past where he had thrown the ball and get in position. Walker squeezed the pigskin by the white laces and lined his shoulders up with the target just like Quinn had done. Quinn didn't know how he was going to throw the ball, though. A quarterback needed a lot of power from his legs to make a long pass. Walker's bad leg wouldn't let him push off much. He'd have to launch the ball almost totally with the strength of his arm.

Walker balanced on his one good leg, pulled the ball back, and thrust his muscular arm forward. The ball shot through the crisp autumn air like an arrow: ten ... twenty ... thirty ... forty ... fifty yards. Despite the tire swaying gently in the breeze, the ball found the black target and zipped right through the hole.

Quinn was speechless.

"Not bad, eh?" Walker said, regaining his balance.

"That was awesome! The tire was half a football field away and you nailed it. I didn't think you had a chance."

"That's what the doctors said, too. After the accident."

"Is that why there's something wrong with your leg?" Quinn asked.

"You got it."

Quinn raised his eyebrows. "Was it bad?"

"You could say that. Head-on car crash doing one hundred kilometres an hour on an icy highway."

Quinn cringed.

"A sharp piece of metal from the car sliced into my leg. There was a lot of blood. The doctors didn't think I'd live, let alone walk again."

"But you did. I mean, you do," Quinn said.

"Best I can."

"Your parents must be proud of you."

"Yeah, my mom is always saying that things may be a little tougher for me. But if I work hard enough, I can still achieve what I want."

"What about your dad? Has he been teaching you to throw like that?"

Walker paused. "He was behind the wheel. Killed instantly."

Quinn couldn't speak. He didn't know what to say to a guy who had lost his dad. After a minute, a few words tumbled out. "So, uh, that's why you can't walk so well?"

"Yeah, that's it."

"I bet your leg doesn't look so good underneath those jeans," Quinn said.

"Well, it's the only one I've got, so I think it looks pretty good." Walker hobbled over from the yard and sat on the front steps. "Do you want to see?"

Quinn didn't know what to say. The accident sounded terrible. He'd never laid eyes on a leg that had been in a deadly car crash before. The most he'd ever seen was his own leg with a bruise or a cut after a game.

"O-k-a-a-y . . ."

As Walker started to pull up his pant leg, Quinn couldn't believe what he saw. Instead of coming face to face with a big scar on Walker's shin, Quinn was staring at a shiny steel shaft. It was as if Walker was part bionic, like some kind of Transformer or superhero.

Then came the moment that Quinn would never forget. When Walker finished rolling up his jeans to his knee, he pulled the bottom part of his leg . . . right . . . off!

Quinn just about fell over.

Walker held the leg in one hand to show him. It had a white Nike running shoe attached to a metal shaft on one end and a black fibreglass, bendable knee joint that attached to his thigh on the other.

"When you said your leg was hurt, I never guessed it was . . ."

Walker nodded as he connected the leg back to his knee. "Yeah, the only way to save my life was to cut off my leg."

Quinn winced. "But you're okay now, right?"

"I'm good," Walker said. "So good, I feel like doing a few math problems. How about you?"

Quinn smiled and opened the front door for his friend. "You can start by explaining that pass you just tossed."

"It was one of the best parabolas I've ever thrown," Walker said with a grin.

11 THE MAGICIAN

"I put another chair in your bedroom upstairs," Quinn's mom said, standing on the first step of the staircase. "Walker can use it while you study."

Quinn shot Walker a concerned look. "I'm not sure we'll be going upstairs. Walker can't . . ."

"Upstairs is fine with me," Walker said, cutting Quinn off. "Lead the way."

Quinn looked behind him as he started up the stairs. Walker held on to the railing and took one step at a time. He was at the top in a flash.

"Sweet room," Walker said, eyeing the beanbag chair shaped like a football and the life-sized posters on the wall. "Tom Brady, Peyton Manning, Ricky Ray . . ."

"You know your quarterbacks." Quinn grinned. "Pull up a chair."

"I know my math, too," Walker said, taking a *Math 9* textbook from his backpack.

"Where should we start?" Quinn asked.

Walker cracked open the book and pointed to the first page.

"Chapter one? You must be kidding!" Quinn blurted out in dismay.

"Starting at the beginning is the best way to make sure you understand the basics."

"I know that stuff," Quinn said. "It's just that when we have a test, I freeze up."

"You panic," Walker said.

"Yeah, sweaty, heart-pounding panic."

"After I get through with you, you'll know math so well you'll never break a sweat again."

The two boys sat side by side and got down to some serious studying.

Walker pulled out a piece of paper and drew a long curve on it.

"That's just like the curve Mrs. Devlin drew on the blackboard," Quinn said.

"And that curve is called a . . . ?"

"Parabola," Quinn said.

"Does that smooth curve remind you of anything?" Walker asked.

Quinn smiled. "Yeah, what I wish all my passes looked like."

"The only reason they don't is because you lose focus and get rattled."

"Tell me about it," Quinn said. "Sometimes when the heat's on, I panic and don't think about what I'm doing. The ball either goes too high or too low, or it wobbles."

Quinn tensed up just thinking about throwing a bad pass.

"What if I said there was a trick you could use so that never happened again?

"I'd say you were a magician."

"Next time you throw a pass, imagine the path of the ball," Walker said, closing his eyes.

"So, I just have to picture the ball curving like a parabola to Carter or Jordan?"

"That's it," Walker said. "Focus on that and you'll never throw another wounded duck."

"I wish I could use the same trick in math exams," Quinn said. "In the middle of a test I'll get distracted and start thinking about other stuff — Emma, the game, what I'm having for dinner . . ."

"You can," Walker said. "If another thought pops into your head just block it out. You'll complete your test just like you'll complete your passes. Focus will make you better at math and playing quarterback."

Quinn leaned back in his chair. "How did you ever figure all this out?"

"I wasn't always that good at math," Walker said. "Until I got a chance to spend more time on it."

"How much more time?"

"About as much time as it takes to learn how to walk again."

Quinn nodded. "You mean, after your accident?"

"When you're lying in a hospital bed with only one leg, you've got nothing but time. I didn't want to feel sorry for myself, so I pulled out my books and focused on math instead."

Quinn was amazed by Walker's determination. If he had lost his leg, he just would have been sad and played video games in a dark room all day.

After half an hour there was a knock on the door. Quinn's dad popped his head around the door frame. "Anyone need a break? I brought a bag of chips and a couple of Cokes."

Quinn grit his teeth. "That doesn't sound very healthy. We're athletes, you know. And we've got work to do."

Quinn's dad closed the door, taking the snacks with him.

"My dad eats too much junk food. I don't know what he was thinking."

"I think he was trying to be nice," Walker said.

"I wish he'd quit being so nice and leave me alone. He's always, you know, *around*. Right when I'm in the middle of stuff."

Quinn's hand shot up to cover his mouth but the words had already escaped. He wished he could push rewind and take back what he had blurted out.

"I'll make you a deal," Walker said after a moment. "I'll turn you into a math magician if you promise to never get tired of having your dad around."

Emma was right, thought Quinn. Sometimes I really do think only about myself.

He gave Walker an apologetic nod.

"Deal."

12 BOILING POINT

The cheerleading squad was already on the field. Just like the football team, they had to practice, too. The girls had formed a line in the end zone and were clapping, kicking, and dancing through their routine. Quinn squinted into the afternoon sun. He could see Emma dressed in her red-and-white uniform. She was standing in front of Prita and the other four members of the group. Quinn felt an ache in his stomach like he had eaten a bad piece of pepperoni pizza. Emma had been avoiding him all week. This was as close as he'd been able to get to her.

Quinn took a break from stretching his legs and scoped out the field. He could see Walker and the other new guys spread out on the grass doing their warm-up exercises. He didn't know if the Rebels were any better but at least they had more players now.

Coach waved in the team. "You were lucky to squeak out a win in the last game. Remember, we can't take any team for granted. Our next opponents are tough. Going up against Rockport this Thursday will be a real challenge." Coach took a few steps toward Quinn and Luke. "The offence isn't moving the ball like it should be. The quarterbacks and receivers have to know their plays inside out."

"At least *I* know my plays," Luke said under his breath.

Quinn burned. Last game he forgot a signal for one of the plays. He told Braden to snap the ball on a wrong number, causing an offside penalty against the Rebels. Luke wasn't going to let him — or Coach — forget it.

"That's enough, Chambers," Coach said. "Mistakes happen. The important thing is to recover, which Brown did. He threw a great pass to Washington on the very next play."

Luke glared at Quinn. "He's not the only one who can throw a great pass."

Coach crossed his powerful arms against his suit jacket. "You're on a team, Chambers. You have to support your teammates. And Brown isn't just any teammate, he's the other quarterback. You two guys need to work together. Be role models for the rest of the team."

Coach checked his clipboard and barked out orders. "I want the defence to do some tackling drills and the offence to practise blocking. Meanwhile, I've got a special assignment for Brown, Chambers, Parker, and Woods."

Quinn eyed Luke and Braden, wondering what the drill might be. He didn't trust either one. Putting the two of them together was just asking for trouble.

"Now that Woods is on the team he'll be holding the ball for Hundal when he kicks field goals and the extra points after touchdowns," Coach said. "But Woods has to learn how it's done from the pros. I want you two to show him the proper technique for handling the ball after Parker snaps it."

The four players positioned themselves in front of the goalposts that reached high into the sky. Emma, Prita, and the other cheerleaders were still practising in the end zone. Quinn wished they were far away at the other end of the field. He had a hard time concentrating with Emma around.

Braden gently hiked the ball to Quinn, who demonstrated how to hold it on the ground with one finger on top, ready to be kicked.

"See, nothing to it," Quinn said. "Now you give it a try."

Walker eased himself down on one knee and positioned himself a few paces behind Braden. Quinn noticed he hadn't put on regular knee-length football pants. He was still wearing his long red sweatpants to hide his artificial leg.

Walker signaled for the ball. "Blue . . . forty-two . . . hut!"

This time Braden hiked the ball as hard as he could, sending a low rocket screaming toward Walker. The ball blasted through his hands.

"Just like I thought," Luke said. "You can't catch."

"Yeah, I gave you the ball like I was handing it to a baby." Braden laughed.

Quinn's jaw clenched. "Chill, guys. We all saw what Braden did. No one could have caught that bullet."

Luke wasn't about to shut up. "You're a gimpy loser, Walker. You can't run. You can't hold onto the ball. You wear those stupid sweatpants. You're no use to us. The only thing you're good for is tutoring math morons like Quinn."

The rage that had been building inside Quinn over the past week erupted like a volcano.

He launched himself like a missile, knocking Luke to the ground. The rival quarterback recovered and leaped to his feet, ready to battle. Quinn delivered the first blow, hitting Luke smack against the head. Luke came right back with a solid punch to the chest.

Fists continued to fly, each boy hammering against the other. Despite the flurry of punches, little damage was actually being done. Helmets and pads protected the players from the pounding.

"Break it up!" Braden shouted. The stocky centre tried to pull the boys apart but they were too strong.

In seconds, the rest of the team had come running and circled the grudge match. Some of the players cheered for one quarterback or the other. No one, however, was willing take the risk of stepping in to stop the fight.

Quinn looked away for a split second. He saw a blur of faces . . . Carter . . . Jordan . . . Braden . . . Emma.

Emma? What would she think? Quinn knew she hated violence. She wouldn't even watch a hockey game on TV with him because of the fighting. Now she was standing just a few feet away from a knock-down dogfight.

Emma wasn't the only cheerleader who had raced over.

"Leave my boyfriend alone!" Prita screamed.

Her arms whirled like windmills as she tried to break through the ring of players and attack Quinn. It took the strength of two big Rebels linemen to hold her back.

Then, just as suddenly as the fight began, it was over. Both boys dropped their fists. Their chests heaved as they stood glaring at each other. They were like two heavyweight boxers tired after slugging it out for fifteen rounds.

Quinn's rage inside had leaked away. But knowing Emma was in the crowd was too much for him. If she had hated him before, this was going to be the last nail in his coffin. She might never talk to him again.

"Brown! Chambers!"

Quinn recognized the voice without even seeing who called his name. He knew the punching might have ended, but the pain was still to come.

"I don't know how this fight started, but I know

how it's going to end. With each of you meeting me in my office tomorrow morning. Brown, you first, at 8:00 a.m. sharp. I'll see you at half past, Chambers."

Quinn turned to face the voice. "Coach, I was just defending Walker. You can ask him."

"Is that true, Woods?" Coached asked, looking around.

But there was no reply. As Quinn scanned the players he realized Walker wasn't among them. He was gone.

13 HARD DAYS AHEAD

Quinn sat and awaited his fate. Since he had to face Coach first, at least he could tell his side of the story before Luke did. The office was small, only big enough for a desk and one hard wooden chair. When Coach arrived it would be cramped with just the two of them.

Quinn studied the aging team photos that were framed on the wall. He knew the Rebels football team had a long tradition. He felt like he had let down this squad and every one that had come years before. He would try and make it up to the other players in the next game — make it up to all the players except one. He was still mad at Luke for what he'd said about Walker.

The clock ticked away. It was already 8:10 and the wait was killing Quinn.

Finally, the door clicked open behind him and in rushed Coach Miller. He sat at the oak desk and adjusted his tie. He stared at Quinn with dark, steely eyes.

"I'm late for a business meeting so I'm going to make this brief."

"Yes, sir."

"I've asked some of the other players about who started the fight. Everyone said you threw the first punch. Is that true?"

"Yes, but —"

Coach cut him off. "When it comes to fighting on a team, there are no buts."

"No, sir."

"I don't doubt that Chambers said something that angered you. But you have to control your temper."

"Yes, sir."

"If the other team sacks you behind the line of scrimmage, do you let it get to you?"

"No, sir."

"Or do you keep calm and throw a pinpoint pass to Washington or Brooks the next play?"

"Yes, sir."

"When you fight against the other team in a game, the referee gives you a penalty," Coach said, pointing at Quinn. "And when you fight with your own team in a practice, the coach gives you an even bigger penalty."

Quinn braced himself. He figured Coach might not let him play against Rockport that afternoon. That would be tough to take but he was ready for it. Absolute worst-case scenario was to sit out two games. But he'd be shocked if he made that move. He didn't think Coach would ever bench one of his quarterbacks for two games.

Coach narrowed his eyes. "You're suspended for three games."

Quinn's heart jumped. "You can't!"

"I can," Coach said, holding up his hand like a stop sign. "Case closed."

Coach didn't want to hear any complaining. This was his courtroom. He was the law.

"You'll be back for the last game of the regular season."

"So, Luke will be the only QB until then?" Quinn asked.

"And maybe even after then," Coach said, locking eyes with Quinn. "I need a quarterback who can stay focused. Not some hothead who might start a fight and cost us the game. Luke's been looking good in practice."

Quinn sat in stunned silence.

Coach wasn't finished. "And don't think you'll get off easy for those three games, either. Since you won't be playing I want you to work twice as hard in practice. When the other guys are doing fifty push-ups, you'll be doing a hundred. When they're running five laps, you'll be running ten. Get the picture?"

Quinn hung his head. "Got it, Coach."

"Before the suspension is over, before you suit up for another game, I need you to do one more thing."

"Yes, sir," Quinn said. He knew he was in no position to disagree with anything Coach said.

"I need you to apologize to Luke."

Quinn bit his lip. He didn't know how or where he was going to tell Luke he was sorry. He didn't even know if he really was sorry.

"Don't get me wrong," Coach said. "He's partly to blame. I won't put up with bullying and he's going to be disciplined, too. But for the good of the team, you two need to clear the air."

"How am I going to do that, Coach? We don't exactly talk anymore."

"I don't know," Coach said. "That's for you to figure out."

Coach thumped both hands flat on the desk to signal the meeting was over. "Any more questions?"

"No, sir."

"Well, I have one," Coach said, getting up to leave. "Where's Woods? Tell him I need him to hold the snaps for the kicker. That used to be Luke's job but now he's our only quarterback. He's going to need a rest. He can't do everything."

"Sure," Quinn said, through gritted teeth. "I'll tell him."

★★★

Quinn didn't have to look far. He went to the one place he knew Walker would be. Where he'd be able to hide away from all the teasing and taunting.

The weight room was only a few steps from Coach's office. Quinn pulled open the glass door and glanced around. He could hear the clanging sounds of heavy weights being lifted and the deep breathing of a powerful athlete. He knew the gym teacher could only be helping one kid so early in the morning. He smiled, knowing it was Walker hard at work pumping iron. And all before the first school bell of the day had rung.

"You split pretty fast after the fight yesterday," Quinn said after the teacher had left.

"Everyone was staring at me. I had to get out of there."

"I called you at home but your mom said you weren't feeling well."

"I wasn't really sick," Walker said.

"I know, but you probably were sick of Luke saying you're a loser who can't catch a snap."

"I'm getting used to it," Walker said, nodding. "But it still hurts. Thanks for standing up for me. No one has ever done that before."

"It was the right thing to do."

"I can't be on the team, though," Walker said, shaking his head. "I can't be the cause of fights. That's too big a distraction. The players have to focus on the game, not some math geek with just one leg."

Quinn sat down on a bench a few feet from Walker and looked him in the eye. "Listen to me. You're not a geek. You work harder than anybody else. You're stronger than anybody else. And you're more focused than anybody else."

"Thanks, but I don't think the rest of the team agrees with you."

"Don't worry. I'm going to take care of that," Quinn said. "Would you mind if I told the guys about your leg at practice this afternoon?"

"I dunno if that's a good idea."

"I think we ought to tell them," Quinn said. "But I understand if you don't want to. The thing is, you deserve to be on the team. I think so and so does Coach. The guys will understand things better if they have the whole story, don't you think?"

Walker considered for a moment and then gave Quinn a fist-bump. "I'll see you there."

"Good. So, about that next math lesson . . . " Quinn said, changing the subject to a problem of his own.

"I thought you were rocking that whole math test thing," Walker kidded.

"Not exactly. Unless you think flunking and getting kicked off the team are rockin' it."

"How about right now?" Walker asked. "I've got a free period to start the day."

★★★

Quinn opened the door to the library and the two boys found an empty table at the back in a quiet study area. For the next half-hour Walker brought him up to speed on every math formula, equation, and graph that had been covered in class since their last lesson at the house.

"This is hard work," Quinn said. "I could use a break."

"Yeah, if only there was someone to bring us a snack," Walker joked.

Quinn smiled. "Yeah, like my dad," he said.

Quinn refocused on his math book. He kept his eyes so glued to the page he barely blinked. He only looked away once and that was to glance out the window. But it was worth every second of not paying attention. Strolling by the library at that very moment was Emma. She pretended not to see Quinn and Walker studying together. But he knew she did.

14 RUMOUR MILL

Quinn arrived at practice before Walker. He had to impress Coach, and suiting up early was one way to crawl back into his good books.

He found his regular spot in the far corner of the change room and started putting on his uniform. He was out of sight but he wasn't alone. Luke and some of the other players were already there.

He could hear Walker's name being thrown around like an old football. Even though there had been a knock-down fight over him, most of the players still didn't know the real reason why.

"I wonder what got into Quinn?" Jordan asked.

"Something must have really ticked him off," Tank said.

"He thinks that new kid should be on the team," Luke said. "But we don't think so, do we?"

"He can't run," Braden agreed.

"He can barely walk," Carter added.

"He's just a cripple," Luke said. "He doesn't deserve to be a Rebel."

Quinn's blood started to boil. But fighting again wasn't going to solve anything. He stepped around a row of lockers and came face to face with the players.

"Want to know why Walker deserves to be on the team?" Quinn asked. He stared down the bench at Braden, Tank, Luke, and the others. "Because he's the toughest guy you'll ever meet. Has anybody else in this room been in a terrible car accident? A crash so awful that it killed your dad and sliced a hunk of steel into you like a giant razor blade? A crash so bloody the doctors had to cut off your leg to save your life? Anybody?"

No one said a word. There was dead silence.

Quinn took a deep breath. "Well, Walker has. But he didn't give up. The doctors gave him an artificial leg and he taught himself how to walk again. Then he built himself up. He spends every day in the weight room so he'll have the strongest arms on the team. He's even stronger than Tank. Walker has more guts than all of us put together, and all he wants is a chance."

Finally, Tank broke the ice. "We didn't know how he hurt his leg."

"It doesn't matter how," Quinn shot back. "He could have been sick or he could have been born like that. No one deserves to be called the names he was called."

Each player hung his head.

"Walker can hold the ball for me to kick any time," Jai said. Carter, Jordan, and the rest of the team nodded. Everyone but Luke.

Quinn swallowed hard. He knew there was one more speech he had to make and it wasn't going to be easy. He took a few steps and stopped in front of Luke.

"The fight was my fault. I totally deserve the three-game suspension for losing my cool. It'll never happen again. I'm sorry."

"Whatevs," Luke said. He looked away, then shot back a glare. "But if Walker is so tough, why didn't he say he has only one leg?"

"Because he's too proud to make excuses."

Quinn wasn't sure if Luke had changed his mind about Walker. But at least everyone knew the truth and once Walker arrived, things would be better. And the team could move on.

★★★

Quinn was wiped out.

True to his word, Coach was bringing the hammer down on both him and Luke. He was doubling up on every fitness drill.

"Brown! Chambers! Drop and give me a hundred push-ups!"

"Quit sucking on those water bottles and give me a hundred sit-ups!"

"Pick yourselves up off the turf and run ten laps!"

Both players stumbled back to Coach after their last circuit of the field. But only Quinn collapsed into a pool of his own sweat, gasping for air. He was paying the price for not being in good shape like Luke.

"How are you feeling, Brown?" Coach asked, looking at Quinn sprawled on the grass.

"Never better," Quinn said, not wanting to admit he was whipped.

"Now that you boys are warmed up, I have a couple more tasks." Coach pointed at Luke. "Since you're our only quarterback while Brown is suspended, I want you to lead the squad in a scrimmage."

"The *only* quarterback is on his way," Luke said, giving Quinn a smirk before jogging away.

Coach turned to Quinn, who still lay on the ground. "And I want you to take Woods, Hundal, and Parker over to that goalpost so they can practise kicking converts."

Quinn couldn't move. His arms and legs were more floppy than Woody, the cartoon character from *Toy Story*.

"Let's go!" Walker said, standing over him. "I never thought I'd be telling *you* to hustle."

"Snap to it," Braden kidded. He hiked the pigskin but Quinn was too worn out to even catch it.

Jai picked up the leather. "Let me carry this heavy ball to make it easier for you," he joked.

Quinn dragged himself across the field to make sure Walker held the ball correctly. It took all his energy just to stand there and watch. The hiker, ball–holder, and kicker all had to work together like a finely tuned machine.

Every snap that Braden made was on the money. Every ball that Walker held was perfectly placed. Every kick that Jai made sailed right through the uprights. Quinn knew he'd never have to check on them again. They were pros.

The sky had darkened to a dull grey. Quinn was relieved. The practice was drawing to an end and he had survived. Barely.

"Bring it in!" Coach shouted. He stood at centre field giving Luke and the rest of the team a pep talk before the next game.

"Pass me the ball!" Luke shouted to Quinn. "If you can get it here." He laughed and turned his back on Quinn, Walker, Braden, and Jai, who still stood by the distant goalpost.

Quinn wanted to throw the ball to Luke and prove he had the stronger arm. But he was way too tired and it was way too far, anyway. It must have been over fifty yards.

"Hand me the ball," Walker said to Quinn.

"What?"

"Hand me the ball, man."

Quinn flipped his friend the pigskin. In one smooth motion, Walker pulled his arm back like a slingshot and fired. The ball took off like a bullet and sailed through the sky, heading straight for Luke's back. Braden and Jai stood speechless, watching the ball hurtle toward its target.

Smack!

Coach stopped talking. The players stopped listening. All eyes shifted to Luke, who lay flattened on the ground.

Braden, Jai, Quinn, and Walker hobbled over to join the team.

"Who threw that? Coach asked, narrowing his eyes.

"I did, Coach," Walker said.

"Quit trying to protect Brown," Coach said. "If Brown threw the ball at Chambers he should own up to it."

"It really was Walker," Braden said.

Coach shook his head in disbelief and smiled. "So, Woods threw the ball half a football field and hit the guy who's been picking on him?"

"You got it," Braden said.

Coach thought for a moment. "That seems fair."

15 HEART-STOPPING

"I was wide open," Carter muttered. He slumped on the Rebels' bench beside Quinn, who was back on the team after his three-game suspension.

The speedy wide receiver had just come off the field with the rest of the offence after the Rebels had failed again to make a first down. The yardsticks hadn't moved ten yards in all of the third quarter.

"All Luke has to do is pass me the ball and I'll catch it, man. These wounded ducks he's throwing are killing us."

Quinn knew Carter shouldn't be dissing the quarterback, even if it was Luke. But Carter was totally frustrated. It seemed unlikely Coach was going to do anything about it, though. Quinn had spent the whole first half riding the pine and it didn't look like he was going to see any action. He knew he had to win back Coach's trust, but how was he going to do that if he never got to play?

Quinn felt bad for himself and worse for his parents,

who had come out to watch his first game back. When they heard about the fight they had grounded him. He wasn't allowed to leave home except for school and football practice. They said the only good thing was that Walker was still tutoring him. But now that he had finished sitting out his three games his parents were eager to see him play.

His mom and dad sat in the bleachers with a Thermos full of hot chocolate on the other side of the field. An angry November wind was blowing from the mountains and they were doing their best to stay warm.

Quinn glanced at the scoreboard: Bayside, 21– Riverbend, 13. If the Rebels didn't score a touchdown and a field goal to pull this one out, they could kiss their chance of playing in the championship game goodbye. During the last three games with Luke as the only quarterback, the Rebels had lost two and won only one. Now they were fighting for their playoff lives to make it into the final. He could see Coach knew it, too. He was stalking the sideline like a tiger. He'd pace, stop, put his hands on his hips, shake his head, then start pacing again.

The Rebels' defence had to keep holding the Broncos and get the ball back. That's exactly what they did. Quinn watched their powerful defensive line sack the Bayside quarterback on second down, forcing the orange shirts to punt. He sagged on the bench, knowing Luke would be going in again.

"Brown!" Coach shouted. "Go in for Chambers. Let's make something happen!"

Quinn jolted into action. Every nerve in his body was electrified. This was his chance. He sprang off the bench and sprinted across the field, strapping on his helmet as he ran. The first play he called in the huddle was a corner-pass pattern to Carter. If he had been getting open, then Quinn was going to find him.

"Red . . . sixteen . . . hut!" Quinn wheeled back from Braden and rolled out to his right. At the same time, Carter was hightailing it straight downfield then cutting toward the right corner of the end zone. Sure enough, he was open. Quinn imagined the flight of the pass just like Walker had told him. He gripped the laces on the ball and fired a perfect spiral that hit Carter right in the hands. He didn't even have to break stride. Carter's speed was no match for the Broncos' defender, and he left him tumbling to the ground in his wake. Touchdown!

Quinn pumped his fist as he sprinted off the field. He high-fived Walker, who was coming on to hold the ball for the convert.

"Nice parabola!" Walker said.

There was only one Rebel who didn't come over to congratulate him on the sideline. Quinn didn't expect Luke to be happy for him but he did expect him to be stoked for the team.

Coach patted Quinn on the shoulder pads.

"Welcome back. We just need a field goal now."

Another drive by the Broncos sputtered. It was half-way through the fourth quarter and Quinn raced back onto the field. He broke from the huddle and stood behind Braden, waiting for the snap. His eyes scanned the Bayside defence for a surprise blitz. He was laser-focused. He started to call the signals . . .

Somewhere in the back of Quinn's brain a siren blared. He tried to shake it off. He didn't want anything distracting him from the game. But the high-pitched whine pulsed louder and louder. There was an ambu-lance somewhere in the distance and it was getting closer and closer.

Focus.

The numbers spilled out of him like he was on autopilot. "Red . . . twenty-two . . . hut . . . hut!" Quinn grabbed the ball and made a hand-off to Tank, who swept around the left side. Once his engine was revved up there was almost no stopping him. After a few powerful steps, the hefty fullback was in high gear. He rumbled for twenty yards, plowing over orange jer-seys until he was finally hauled down at the Broncos' twenty-yard line.

With only thirty seconds to play, the ball was well within Jai's range for a field goal. Knowing that Walker would hold the ball perfectly for the kick, Quinn jogged off the field, confident the Rebels would pull off another last-minute victory.

Every player on the sideline was pointing. Quinn grinned, thinking they were saluting him. But he was wrong. There were no high-fives waiting for him on the bench this time. He turned to see what they were looking at. Across the field, the red lights of an ambulance were flashing near the bleachers. Quinn figured a fan had fallen from the stands and gotten hurt, a broken arm at worst.

Lucky that my mom is sitting near whoever got hurt, he thought. *She's probably in full nurse-mode right now.*

Jai kicked the winning field goal. The final whistle blew. The Rebels and their fans cheered. The team started to file back to the locker room. Quinn scanned the crowd for his parents.

Suddenly, Quinn stood frozen on the sideline. His eyes locked on the emergency unfolding right before him on the other side of the field.

It was like a bad dream. He started walking toward the crimson lights that blazed against the darkening sky. Soon he was running. His legs churned harder than they ever had in the game. Faster and faster he sped. He arrived at his mother's side, gasping for breath.

"It's Dad, isn't it?"

His mother stared at him wide-eyed without saying a word. Her tears spoke for her.

16 HOSPITAL ZONE

Quinn waited just outside the hospital room, his feet glued to the floor, afraid to go in. *What if his dad never woke up? What if he never got to talk to him again?* He peeked around the corner. Clear plastic tubes poked out of his dad's nose. Electrical wires patched to his chest ran to a green digital screen that beeped beside him. His mom sat in a chair beside his father. She was still wearing her blue nurse's uniform.

She looked up, catching his stare. "The tubes are to help your father breathe," she said, waving him in. "The wires are taking his heart rate and blood pressure."

"Dad doesn't look so good," Quinn said, still standing at a distance.

"The doctor said it was a heart attack. That he's still in serious condition and will have to stay in the hospital for a few more days. She said if he doesn't change his diet and start exercising it could happen again. Next time he could even . . ."

"Don't worry, Mom," Quinn said, sitting beside her. "Dad and I can work out together at home. I'll make sure we exercise every day."

Quinn watched his dad's eyes flicker open.

"Welcome back," his mom said. "You had us worried."

"You can't get rid of me that easily," his dad said, smiling weakly. "I'll be my old self soon enough, ready for another big meal after the next game."

Quinn's mom's eyes sharpened. "I'm sure you will, Dwayne, but there'll be no burgers and no fries for you at that meal."

His dad looked around the room at all the wires, tubes, and concerned faces, then shook his head. "This place is way too serious. It's like someone had a heart attack or something. When can I get out?"

"The doctor said they want to monitor you for a few days."

"And then back to work, right?" his dad said. "I've only been here a few hours and I'm bored already."

"Not even close, Dwayne," his mom said. "The doctor wants you to take it easy for a month and then only go back to Canadian Tire part-time."

She gave Quinn a concerned glance. "You're probably starving."

"I haven't had time to think about food. Coach gave me a ride straight here after the game. But now that you mention it, I could go for some eats."

"Why don't you go down to the hospital cafeteria and grab something?" She passed him a ten-dollar bill.

Seeing that his dad had fallen back asleep, Quinn turned for the door. Standing there was someone he hadn't spoken to in weeks.

"I thought you could use a friendly face," Emma said.

"I wasn't sure you'd ever want to see me again."

"Don't be silly," she said. "Oh, and I didn't come here alone."

Quinn's eyes grew wide. That whole feeling of panic he got from math tests swept over him again. Maybe she had brought a new boyfriend? He probably deserved that after the way he had behaved.

"Hey, man, how are you doing?"

"Walker, what are you doing here?" Quinn breathed a sigh of relief and grinned.

Walker returned the smile. "Are you kidding? Hospitals, doctors, nurses, beeping machines . . . this was my life for a long time. I thought you might need someone to explain it all."

Quinn was relieved he didn't have to go through this alone. Knowing that Emma and Walker understood what he was feeling made it easier. He knew he was lucky to have such good friends.

Quinn took Emma by the arm as they walked past the nurses' desk to the elevator.

"I saw the whole thing," Emma said, squeezing his hand. "We were on the other sideline, cheering after the touchdown, when the ambulance roared onto the grass by the bleachers. I could see your mom waving at the two paramedics who came running with their bags. She was panicked! Her face was as white as a ghost's. I knew something must have happened to your dad."

"I should have been watching," Quinn said. "I should have been there to help."

"That's crazy!" Walker said. "You can't blame yourself for not being there. We were in the middle of the a game. Who do you think you are — Superman?"

"No." Quinn grinned at Emma. "But if I was, you'd be Lois Lane."

"And you know even a superhero's girlfriend doesn't like fighting." She raised an eyebrow.

"I know," Quinn said, sheepishly. "I should have controlled myself but if you had heard the terrible things Luke was saying about Walker's leg, you might have snapped, too."

Walker nodded. "It was bad. But Quinn stood up for me."

"I heard," Emma said. "But punching Luke was still a stupid thing to do. Then again, I would have been more upset if you hadn't defended Walker. I'm proud of you for that."

Stepping into the cafeteria, Quinn scanned the

menu board. He was about to order for Emma like he always did but stopped. "What would you like?"

"A bowl of soup sounds good," she said, smiling. "And thanks for asking."

17 THE DECISION

Quinn sat alone in the locker room, staring at the cold, tiled floor. He had arrived early to try and concentrate on the big game ahead. But every time he pictured a play in his head, all he could see was his dad lying in the hospital bed. He knew his teammates were counting on him. He had to focus.

In just over an hour, the Rebels would take on their archrivals to battle for the championship. They had narrowly beaten Sprucewood in the opening game of the season, but the Spartans had made a comeback of their own in the past few weeks. They were now the hottest team in the league and had rolled over Rockport to qualify for the final.

Even though the room was empty, Quinn could still hear voices. At first he thought he was imagining them. *Maybe the pressure is getting to me*, he thought. Soon he realized the talking wasn't coming from his mind but from the coach's office next door.

"You still need to choose your quarterback, Coach.

I think it should be Quinn," a man said. Quinn listened closely. The voice sounded familiar.

"I'm not sure, Coach," the second man said. "He's had some trouble this year. Keeps losing focus. Can't keep his head in the game. It's a tough decision between him and Luke."

Two coaches? Quinn thought to himself. *What's with that?* The first coach sounded a lot like old Coach Gordon. Maybe he was back to pick players for the all-star team?

"Team Alberta needs a QB with a good head on his shoulders who can scramble and pass," Coach Gordon said.

"You may only see one boy in action today," Coach Miller said.

"Just one?"

"I'm keeping my decision for who's starting at quarterback a secret until game time," Coach Miller said. "If that QB doesn't perform, I'll put in the other. But only *if*. That's the way we've been doing it all season and that's the way we're doing it today."

Quinn wondered who Coach Miller would choose to start the game at quarterback. But he didn't have time to think about it. He heard the click of the door opening. "I'll be in the bleachers taking notes," Coach Gordon said. "Good luck to the Rebels. May the best team win."

One by one, the rest of the Rebels started streaming

into the locker room. They were pumped. After last game's big comeback, every player thought Quinn would be the starting quarterback and pounded fists with him.

"Let's do this!" Carter whooped.

"Ready to throw some more touchdowns?" Jordan asked.

Tank pretended to take a hand-off. "Just give me the ball, and I'll take care of the rest."

Most of his teammates asked about the game. Only one asked what was really on his mind — his dad.

"I know how you feel," Walker said, taking a seat on the bench beside him. "The thought of losing your father can really mess with your head."

Quinn nodded and just wished he was as psyched for the game as the other guys. His dad had still looked grey and weak when Quinn saw him in the hospital the previous day.

That was why this game was so important. Quinn thought that if the Rebels could win the championship and he could make the all-star team, then somehow that would make his dad feel better. He had to play the game of his life, if he got to play. The pressure was on and the ball hadn't even been kicked off yet. Quinn did his best to smile.

Coach Miller walked briskly into the middle of the room. All eyes were on him. He was dressed in new battle gear for the big tilt. He wore a black business suit, which was no surprise. But over top was a faded red jersey with a big number twenty-two on the front. It reminded Quinn of the uniforms he had seen in the old Rebels photographs.

"Listen up, men," Coach Miller said, casting his eyes around the room. "I don't have to tell you this is the biggest game of the year. But we're going to be in tough against Sprucewood. They're not the same team we beat earlier in the year."

"Are the rumours true?" Carter asked.

Coach nodded. "You may have heard the Spartans have a new player who just moved here from down south. Well, it's true. His name is Deon Jones and he wears number thirty-three. He's a defensive back from New York with blazing speed who can track down even the fastest receivers. No one has scored against him yet."

"Don't worry, Coach," Jordan bragged. "He hasn't seen guys with jets like Carter and me."

"The Spartans can be beaten," Coach said. "But it means every one of you has to give his all and sacrifice for the team. Every one of you has to be razor sharp and focused on every play. We can't be worrying about girlfriends, the latest tune on your playlist, or family problems."

While Coach didn't add *worrying about fathers with heart attacks* to his list, he might as well have.

"That's why I'm choosing Chambers to start at quarterback," Coach said. "The only thing on his mind is this game. He's taken us to victory once before and he can do it again. But he can't do it alone. I'm asking each of you to give Chambers your full support."

The room fell into an uneasy silence. Quinn looked over at Jordan, who raised his eyebrows in disbelief. Carter hung his head as if the game were over before it had even started. Then Quinn shot a glance toward Braden. He was still Luke's best friend. The hefty centre jumped up from the bench with a determined look on his face. "You can lead us, Luke. Let's go, Rebels!"

Quinn was disappointed but he couldn't blame Coach for the decision. Even he had to admit his head wasn't totally into the game like it should have been. Quinn tied up the laces on his cleats and flew onto the field with the other Rebels. He just wasn't soaring quite as high.

18 WOUNDED

Led by their pompom-shaking cheerleaders, the Sprucewood Spartans football team charged onto the Riverbend field. Quinn stood by the Rebels' bench and watched the swarm of black jerseys form a giant huddle. The players were so jacked with energy, they jumped up and down like they were on pogo sticks. The Spartans didn't look like the same team the Rebels had come back to beat in the season opener. They weren't thinking about the past. They were totally focused on beating the Rebels right here and now. There was no fear in their eyes today.

The Spartans were on a roll. They had crushed their opponents in their last three outings, giving up only a single touchdown each game. Quinn watched them warming up on the field and started to see why. Loping by his teammates like they were standing still was a muscular player with number thirty-three on his uniform. While the other Spartans were running at full tilt, Deon was only jogging.

This guy has wheels.

Quinn tried not to feel sorry for himself. But every time he looked across the field, he saw the bleachers where his dad had fallen to the ground with a heart attack. Every time he looked at his team, he saw Luke warming up to be the starting quarterback. Every time he thought about getting chosen for the all-star team, he knew Coach Gordon would be scouting, wondering why he wasn't playing.

Walker eased up beside him on the sideline. "Don't let this get to you, man."

"I had a lot riding on this game," Quinn said. "And now I'm not even going to be in it."

Walker stared straight ahead. "Things don't always go your way. You just have to deal with it."

Quinn glanced at his friend, knowing that was just what he had done. Knowing that Walker had fought through tough times made him feel better.

"You'll get your chance," Walker said.

Quinn nodded but he wasn't so sure.

The only bright spot of the afternoon for Quinn was watching Emma lead the Rebels' cheerleading squad in front of the bleachers. The stands were packed with students who had stayed after school and parents who had left work early to watch. Quinn didn't bother looking for his mom and dad like he usually did since he knew they were at the hospital.

Coach Miller called the team in for his pre-game

pep talk. "We've won the coin toss and chosen to receive the opening kickoff. That means our offence will get the ball first. The game plan is to start with our running attack and then add passing plays when the Spartans aren't expecting them. We want to keep our passes away from Deon Jones as much as possible. So, Chambers, don't throw in the direction of number thirty-three. Got it?"

"Got it, Coach!" Luke shouted, strapping on his helmet.

The Spartans lined up across the field twelve men strong and booted the opening kick. The Rebels caught the towering drive and ran the ball back to their own thirty-yard line. Luke led the offence onto the field and quickly called a play in the huddle. Quinn watched the starting quarterback hand off the ball to Tank. With his wide shoulders and powerful legs, Tank should have been able to blast through the Spartans' defensive line. No such luck. The bruising fullback was jammed up at the line of scrimmage and held for no gain.

It was second and ten. Luke stood behind Braden, his trusty centre, calling the signals. Braden snapped the pigskin and Luke pitched the ball to Tank again. This time the play was a sweep around the right end. The result was no better. Tank was nailed by a Spartan linebacker just as he was picking up steam. He managed to gain only three yards.

Quinn heard the whoops of the Spartans cheering

from their bench. The black jerseys had won the first battle of the afternoon. The Rebels were forced to punt the ball.

Sprucewood made it look easy. Led by their general at quarterback, the Spartans marched straight into Rebels territory like a powerful army. Hand-off to the left. Pass to the right. Draw up the middle. The Spartans left a string of red jerseys missing tackles, swatting at passes, and falling helplessly to the ground. It was a battlefield covered with Rebel bodies.

Quinn shook his head as the Sprucewood halfback raced around the right side into the Rebels' end zone, scoring the first points of the game. The Spartans circled around the speedy running back and high-fived each other. It wouldn't be the last time they celebrated.

The Rebels lined up to receive the Spartans' next kickoff. Coach Miller tried to rally his troops. "Let's go, Big Red!" he shouted from the sideline.

But the big red machine wasn't going anywhere. After catching the kick deep in his own territory, the Rebels' return man tried running up the sideline, but a chasing Spartan made a shoestring tackle. The ref marked the ball on the twenty-yard line.

Luke and the Rebels' offence went to work. Quinn knew the game plan was to run the ball but he thought the Spartans would be expecting the same strategy. And they were. The first play Luke called was a draw running play up the middle. Luke dropped back, pretending to pass, then handed the ball off to Tank. Three steps later, he was met by a black wall, otherwise known as the Spartan front four. Tank got bulldozed and picked up only two yards. It was second down and eight. The Rebels had one more chance before they had to punt.

"Red Rebel!" Coach Miller shouted.

That was the Rebels' code for "pass." Quinn watched Luke break the huddle, knowing he'd be throwing the ball on the next play. It was the right call for Coach to make, but Quinn wasn't sure Luke could pull it off.

Luke grabbed the snap from Braden and rolled out to his right, looking downfield for a receiver. Carter looked wide open. Everyone on the Rebels bench jumped up, expecting a big catch — a catch that would move the Rebels closer to a touchdown to tie the score.

Luke looked toward Carter, who had no Spartans covering him, and threw the ball. "Uh-oh," Quinn said under his breath. Instead of flying in a tight spiral, the pigskin wobbled, taking longer than normal to get to Carter. In the blink of an eye, the play changed. While the pass floated slowly through the sky, a Spartan defensive back had time to dart over and pick off the ball.

Quinn didn't even have to look at the player's number. The flash with number thirty-three on his jersey had intercepted the ball and was headed the other way. First, he beat a couple of Rebels with nifty shake 'n bake moves. Then, Deon Jones high-stepped into the

Rebels' end zone for a touchdown. He celebrated by spinning the ball on the turf like a top.

Sprucewood hadn't finished their attack against Riverbend. They scored another touchdown just before the end of the second quarter. The only good news was that their kicker missed the extra point. With the war half over, the wounded Rebels dragged their tired bodies over to the sideline and looked up at the scoreboard: Spartans, 20–Rebels, 0.

19 THE SPEECH

Quinn sat hunched on the bench. He hadn't moved for the entire first half. There was no need to. He wasn't playing and it didn't feel like he was ever going to play again. Coach had barely glanced his way — it was like he couldn't see him at all. He felt like a ghost.

For most of the game, Quinn stared down at his cleats, sick of watching the massacre taking place on the field. Even when he did look up, all he saw was disaster — Luke throwing an interception or the unstoppable Spartans marching down the field to score another touchdown. It sucked. The only thing that halted the pain was the ref blowing the whistle to end the first half.

"Man, this is the worst game we've ever played," Carter said in disgust. He yanked off his helmet and threw it to the turf, where it rolled to a stop at Quinn's feet.

"It wasn't just bad, it was brutal," Tank said, limping to the sideline. "I barely got to touch the ball."

Walker, Jai, and the other players who hadn't seen any action sat next to Quinn. Luke, Braden, and Jordan sprawled on the ground with Carter, Tank, and the rest of the Rebels. They had all been taking a pounding at the hands of the Spartans. Uniforms were grass-stained and muddy. Muscles were sore. Hopes were bruised. No one was talking.

Coach Miller's hulking frame paced in front of the shot-down Rebels during the ten-minute halftime break. His jaw was tightly clenched but he looked more determined than angry. He scanned down the line from Carter to Jordan to Tank. "How many guys think we're beat?"

More silence.

"Well, anyone who thinks we don't have a chance can head back to the locker room right now."

No one moved.

"He knows what he's talking about," Coach Gordon said.

Quinn was so focused on his own troubles that he hadn't seen his old coach creep up beside the bench. Coach Gordon was still holding the clipboard he had used for taking scouting notes during the first half of the game. Quinn figured it must have been filled with all-star recommendations for all the Spartan players at this point.

Coach Gordon stood beside Coach Miller and spread out his arms, ready to speak. "Twenty years ago when I first started coaching here at Riverbend, I had a young quarterback. Let's call him Mike. Mike had every tool in the quarterback tool box. He was big and strong and could throw the ball like a bullet. But what made Mike so good wasn't the size of his body; it was the size of his heart. Mike never believed his team was out of a game. That we were too far behind. That we could ever lose. Yeah, sure, sometimes we did come up short, but it was never for lack of trying. And it's not like he never got mad — but he would never throw a tantrum or anything."

Carter looked sheepish as he picked up the helmet he had hurled aside.

"Instead he became laser-focused and got the job done. All the other players knew it, too. They trusted their leader and followed him into battle, willing to sacrifice for the team. They were special years. You can see the results still displayed on the awards wall by the gym."

Quinn was mesmerized by Coach Gordon's story. He wasn't looking down anymore. He pictured the big, gold trophies that sat behind the glass cabinet and the photograph of the quarterback who had won all those championships. And he realized that Coach Gordon was talking about number twenty-two: Coach Mike "the Rifle" Miller.

Coach Gordon didn't say another word. He put his hand on the shoulder of Coach Miller's faded red jersey and headed for the stands to watch the second half of the game.

Coach Miller took a deep breath and stepped among the wounded Rebel players. "Yeah, we're way behind," he said, stopping in front of Luke. "But I'm not blaming anyone except myself."

Luke hung his head, knowing he had disappointed Coach by tossing those interceptions.

"But one thing I've learned in business is that if something isn't working, you can't keep doing it the same way and expect things to get better. You have to change it."

"What are we going to change?" Braden asked.

"Every time we run the ball they stop us," Tank said.

Carter shook his head. "Every time we pass they shut us down."

Coach's dark eyes hardened. "That's the way the first half went but it's not the way the second half is going to go. Brown, you're going in for Chambers. Let's see what you've got."

Had he heard Coach right? Was he coming off the bench at last? A surge of adrenaline raced through Quinn's body. He sprang to his feet. No one else stayed sitting on the bench or lying on the ground, either. Every tired, beaten-up, almost-defeated body stood up. Coach Gordon had gathered the wood and Coach Miller had lit the fire. Now it was up to Quinn to make sure the flames burned for the rest of the game.

There was still a lot of fight left in the Rebels. Quinn knew the odds were stacked against them. But he knew Coach Miller wasn't about to give up. And neither was he.

"This is your chance," Walker said, nodding to his friend.

Quinn clicked the chinstrap on his red helmet.

"Let's do this."

20 THE BIG BREAK

Quinn knelt on one knee in the middle of the huddle. In most games, he wouldn't say anything other than just calling the play. But this was no regular game.

"We're down by three touchdowns. If we want to be champions we have to score almost every time we get the ball." Quinn's teammates hung on every word. "That means we're going to the air. Carter and Jordan, get ready to fly."

Quinn clapped his hands to break the huddle. The five burly members of the Rebels' offensive line stood nose to nose against the hefty Spartans' front line. The players lowered into their powerful three-point stances and readied for combat.

Quinn crouched behind Braden and stared over his hunched back into an opposing player's eyes. They were deep-set under a black helmet and wire facemask. Quinn saw no fear, only gritty determination, as they waited for the snap of the ball. Anyone who thought Sprucewood was going to roll over now that they had a big lead would be dead wrong.

"Red . . . twenty-two . . . hut!"

Quinn grabbed the snap from Braden and back-pedalled into the pocket. The Spartan front four dug their cleats hard into the muddy turf and broke through the Rebels' defensive line. Quinn scrambled to his left, buying time to find a receiver downfield. Even though there was a huge black jersey breathing down his neck, Quinn kept his focus. He pictured the pass sailing through the air like a perfect parabola. He cocked his arm and fired to Jordan, streaking down the middle. The ball took off from his fingers like a bullet and hit Jordan right in the hands in full flight.

Quinn watched his talented wide receiver blaze fifty yards into the Spartan end zone. The ref shot both arms straight into the air, signalling a touchdown. Jordan didn't jump up and down, do a dance, or celebrate. He handed the ball straight to the ref. The Rebels didn't have a second to waste.

Walker hobbled on to hold the ball for Jai, who easily kicked the brown leather through the goalposts. The extra point was good. Score: Spartans, 20–Rebels, 7.

The Rebels were pumped. In the first half, the Spartans had run all over them. But now their defence was invincible. Every play the Spartans ran was met by a group of gang-tackling red jerseys. A single Rebel might not have been able to bring down a Spartan, but against an entire army, a runner had no chance.

The Spartans were forced to punt the ball back to the Rebels over and over.

Three series of downs later the Rebels were on the march again. On this drive, Quinn mixed up his calls and switched between running and passing plays. Tank had just carried the ball for a fifteen-yard gain and now it was Carter's turn to hit pay dirt from the Spartans' twenty-yard line.

Quinn called for him to run straight then cut toward the flag that marked the corner of the end zone. Quinn and Carter had practised the flag pattern over and over again until their timing was perfect.

Carter bolted from the line of scrimmage. Quinn squeezed the pigskin, stepped back into the pocket, and waited until his receiver was about to break for the corner.

The Spartan defensive back was blanketing Carter with tight coverage and Quinn knew his pass would have to be perfect. He shifted his weight onto his back foot, cocked his arm, and rifled the ball. Carter kept running at full speed until the ball caught up to him just inside the flag. He reached up and held it tight in his outstretched hands while crashing to the ground.

Touchdown! Quinn raced into the end zone to high-five Carter. The two grinning players jumped into the air, hurling themselves at each other in a shoulder-bump.

Walker's strong hands held the ball for Jai as he booted it through the uprights for the convert. Score: Spartans, 20–Rebels, 14.

Quinn and Coach Miller stood side by side at the bench, waiting for the Rebels to get the ball back.

"Just one more touchdown to pull into the lead," Coach said.

"I think we can do it."

"Think?" Coach asked.

"I *know* we can do it."

"That's more like it," Coach said. "Sometimes the pressure gets to you, Brown. And with your dad's heart attack and everything, I was just worried you might lose your focus."

"Don't be, Coach. Walker has straightened me out."

"Woods? What could a kid with a bad leg teach *you* about football?"

"Plenty, Coach. He's the most focused person you'll ever meet. He's taught me how to block everything out and concentrate on what I'm doing."

The Spartans weren't about to let the Rebels come back without a fight. They had regrouped and were driving down the field. The Riverbend defence finally held, forcing the Spartans to punt. They kicked the ball all the way down to the Rebel ten-yard line.

Long shadows were creeping across the field. Coach Miller patted Quinn on the back and sent him in with the rest of the offence. The Rebels had won the ball back but they were deep in their own end. It was late in the fourth quarter. Time was running out.

The Rebels huddled in their own end zone. Quinn shot a glance at the clock — just thirty seconds left. Somehow the Rebels had to take the ball one hundred yards and score a touchdown. And he had time for only two plays.

The old Quinn would have started to sweat. What two plays should he call? But the new Quinn stayed cool. Walker had taught him not to panic during math tests. To believe in himself. Nothing could rattle him now.

He called a short-slant pattern to Jordan, hoping his receiver could dash out of bounds to stop the clock.

Quinn stood behind his centre and scanned the Spartan defence. Something looked different but he wasn't sure what. Braden snapped the ball into Quinn's waiting hands and he backpedalled into the pocket. That's when he realized what the Spartans had planned.

A blitz!

Two Spartan defensive backs had snuck up to the line and were now charging full tilt right at him. Quinn wanted to scramble away but there was a black jersey closing in fast from each direction. He was trapped. His only chance was to throw a pass before he became a Spartan sandwich. Quinn put all his weight on his back foot, ready to pass.

That's when disaster struck. The two rushing Spartans crunched Quinn at the same time. He heard something snap and felt a searing pain shoot through his leg. Quinn slumped to the ground, grasping his calf.

The referee blew his whistle, instantly stopping the game. The Rebels gathered around their fallen leader, knowing something was terribly wrong. Even the Spartans looked on with concern. All was quiet. Coach Miller sprinted onto the field and knelt beside his quarterback.

"It's my leg, Coach."

"I know."

"It was our last chance to win," Quinn gasped.

"I know."

Coach gently patted him on the shoulder.

"Let's get you to the sideline."

21 LONG BOMB

"What are we going to do?" Quinn asked, once he was sitting on the bench with his leg propped up in front of him. "There's just one play left."

Coach didn't hesitate. "I'll put in Chambers."

"Luke's arm isn't strong enough," Quinn said, gritting his teeth. "We need someone who can throw the ball long."

"He's all we've got. We gave it our best shot."

Quinn couldn't believe what he was hearing. It sounded like Coach was giving up. There must be another answer.

"Luke isn't the only quarterback we've got," Quinn said, shooting a glance at Coach.

"What are you talking about?"

"We've got Walker."

Coach raised his eyebrows. "But he can't even run."

"Maybe not, but no one can throw the ball farther. Not even me."

Luke was waiting for them on the sideline. He

already had his helmet strapped on.

"I'm ready, Coach."

"Change of plan, Chambers." Coach turned to a lone figure sitting at the end of the bench.

"Woods!

"Yes, sir!"

"How's your arm?"

"Good, sir."

"You're going in for Brown as quarterback."

Every jaw dropped. The entire team was stunned. And then they remembered the practice. The day Walker hit Luke square in the back from fifty yards. The day they saw the power of the new boy's arm. Gradually, their heads stopped shaking and started to nod. All but one.

"You're putting in Walker? Instead of me?" Luke said in stunned disbelief. "He can't even run!"

"He doesn't have to," Coach said. "We need a long bomb."

Walker lowered his chin in a determined clench as he passed. "I won't let you down, Coach."

Quinn watched his friend hobble across the field, the shiny steel of his artificial leg gleaming in the late afternoon sun. Walker no longer wore sweatpants to hide his leg. He didn't care what people thought of him. All he wanted to do was be a football player like everyone else.

Despite the stabbing pain that shot down his own leg, Quinn found the strength for one last shout.

"Hit the tire, man!"

Everyone witnessing the game fell silent. All eyes were on the field. The Rebels on the bench sprang to their feet and rushed to the sideline to watch. The Spartans couldn't believe what they were seeing. Emma and the cheerleaders froze in place and stared. The fans in the stands pointed at the boy shuffling out to the huddle.

Quinn sat on the bench, holding his injured leg, and watched the last play of the game unfold.

The line of scrimmage was deep in Rebel territory. Walker stood behind Braden, getting ready to call the play. Quinn knew he'd be totally focused. Nothing could distract him now. Not the bullying from Luke. Not the memory of losing his dad. He'd be imagining the flight of the ball curving through the air like a parabola, all the way to Carter.

Walker knew the signals and shouted out, "Red ... fifty-five!" That was the long bomb. It was a do-or-die call for last-play situations just like this. Throw the ball as far as you could to the fastest guy on the team.

Braden snapped the ball extra far so that Walker wouldn't have to stumble backwards into the pocket. That would give him more time to throw. His powerful hands grabbed the pigskin. His fingers gripped the laces. He waited as long as he could for his speedy receiver to run down the field.

Quinn saw Carter dash from the line of scrimmage the split second the ball was hiked. He had never seen him run so fast. He sprinted straight down the right side then broke to the middle of the field toward the goalpost. By the time Walker was ready to pass, Carter was already in Spartan territory. That was over fifty yards away!

"No kid can throw that far," Coach said in disbelief.

"Don't count him out," Quinn said.

Coach and Quinn shielded their eyes against the setting sun and held their breath. With the strength gathered from countless days of building up his arms in the weight room, Walker launched the final pass of the game. He threw the football with all his might, collapsing to the ground as it flew out of his grasp. The ball shot from his fingers like a cannon blast sailing through the air in a perfect spiral.

There was only silence from those watching on the sideline. Even Luke was speechless as the ball flew past the yard markers:

Ten.

Twenty.

Thirty.

Forty.

Fifty.

The leather missile carried all the way into Spartan territory. Carter was in full gallop. He reached out his hands and the ball landed sweetly on his fingertips — a perfect bull's eye. Carter tucked the pigskin into the crook of his arm and raced for the end zone, now just forty yards away.

Quinn didn't think anyone could touch him. Coach jumped on top of the bench to get a better look. The Rebel players leaped along the sideline, cheering what had seemed impossible just seconds before.

That was when Quinn saw him. A black-shirted blur from the far side of the field. Number thirty-three had Carter in his sights and was hunting him down. Like a cheetah tracking his prey, Deon Jones was flying across the grass. So great was his speed that his cleats barely touched the earth beneath him.

Quinn knew it was going to be close. Did Carter have enough gas left to reach the end zone? Or would Deon's last-second dash catch him?

The answer came in the blink of an eye. In a last-gasp effort, Deon dove through the air like a super-hero, tackling Carter on the edge of the Spartans' goal line.

The final whistle blew. The players on the field stopped running. The players on the sideline stopped cheering. Quinn and Coach could only stare. Riverbend's last chance to win the championship game was over. Despite the greatest pass in the history of Rebels football, the dream had come to an end on the one-yard line.

22 TABLES TURNED

Mrs. Devlin swooped down the aisle from her perch at the front of the class.

"A much better effort, Quinn." She handed back his math test, with a bright red "80%" in the top right-hand corner. "You must be doing something right."

Quinn grinned, knowing that "something" was Walker. "I've got a good tutor."

"I bet you do," the math teacher chirped as the bell rang. "That's it for today."

As usual, Luke was in a hurry to be the first one out of the class. He raced by Quinn, almost tripping over his outstretched leg.

"Watch it, Gimpy!" Luke said.

Quinn would have pulled in his leg except for one crucial factor — he had a cast on it. Quinn didn't expect an apology. It was Luke, after all.

Walker looked down the aisle at Quinn. "Race you to the cafeteria."

"Very funny," Quinn said, picking up his crutches

from the floor. "You'd leave me in your dust."

Quinn swung his leg between the crutches and moved up the aisle, careful not to bang his cast against the desks. He reached the door and looked down the hallway. This time he was the one hobbling behind.

"What's the rush?" he called. "I have only one speed now — and that's *slow*."

Walker waited in the middle of the hall. He smiled and shook his head. "Do I have to give you crutch lessons, too?"

Quinn and Walker continued their slow parade, following their noses to the cafeteria. Quinn breathed in deeply. "Ah, the best part of the school day."

The two boys stood at the entrance and scanned the crowded room. Carter, Jordan, Tank, and Jai were digging into their brown bags and sharing a joke at one table. But it was a girl sitting by herself that caught their attention. Quinn and Walker shuffled over to join their friend.

Emma jumped up from her seat. "Can I help you with the chair?"

Quinn hopped up and down on one foot as he fumbled with his crutches. "Does it look like I need help?" He laughed. Now that he was injured, Quinn appreciated Emma's kindness even more.

"I'm starving," Quinn said, carefully lowering himself into his seat. "A guy can really work up an appetite trying to get around on these sticks all day."

"Your stomach can wait," Emma said. "Tell Walker the good news, first."

"What's up?" Walker asked, sitting down.

"Looks like my dad is going to be okay. The doctor said as long as he eats better and exercises, he can make a full recovery."

"I'm happy for you," Walker said. "That's the best news a son can get."

Quinn paused. He knew Walker would be thinking about his own dad.

"There's something else. You know that league all-star team I was hoping to make?"

"I guess breaking your leg put an end to that," Walker said.

"Yes and no," Quinn said. "I got a letter from Coach Gordon yesterday saying I would have been chosen as the quarterback if I hadn't busted my leg."

"That's too bad."

"But the good news is they're making me honourary captain of the team, so I get to go to the game in Toronto!"

"You totally deserve it," Walker said. "I'm sure those two touchdowns you threw before getting injured were all Coach Gordon needed to see. They were awesome."

"Thanks, but they were nothing compared to that long bomb you tossed. I've never seen anything like it. Not even by the pros on TV."

"It was one of my better passes," Walker said, without

bragging. "I only wish we could have scored. Maybe if I had thrown it a few yards farther."

"It wasn't your fault," Quinn said, shaking his head. "We had no chance, but you gave us one. Even though we lost the game you're still a hero, man."

"I'm sure no one else thinks that," Walker said.

Quinn looked up to see four surprise visitors approaching behind Walker. "You don't have to take my word for it."

One by one, Carter, Jordan, Tank, and Jai pounded fists with the last-play hero.

"I feel like I let you down," Carter said. "If I had better wheels I could have scored."

Tank patted Walker on the shoulder. "The next time we need to throw the ball half a football field, we know who can do it."

"If I can, Quinn can," Walker said. "Quinn Brown is your real QB."

The four Rebels knuckle-bumped their seated teammates one more time before heading off.

Listening to Walker made Quinn realize he could be a better player. "I'm going to train harder next year. Build up my arms to be stronger, too. I want to be the best quarterback in the league. But to throw the long bomb, I'm going to need some passing lessons."

"Sounds like you'll need a teacher for passing math *and* footballs," Walker kidded.

"Speaking of passing math," Emma broke in, "I've

got a big test coming up and I could sure use some help. Know any good tutors?"

Quinn shot a smile at Walker. "I think I might."

Walker checked the lineup for buying pizza. "So, who's hungry?"

"I'm always ready for a slice," Quinn said, reaching for his crutches. "I'll get some."

Walker waved him off. "Your leg is hurt. Let me get it for you."

CHECK OUT THESE OTHER BASKETBALL STORIES FROM LORIMER'S SPORTS STORIES SERIES:

Bench Brawl
by Trevor Kew

The Helmets and the Gloves have been cross-river rink rivals forever, so when the league decides to merge the two teams to represent their small B.C. town at a big invitational hockey tournament in Vancouver, Luke and his friends are furious. It will take an outsider from Quebec to teach the locals the true meaning of sportsmanship.

Camp All-Star
by Michael Coldwell

Jeff's been invited to an elite basketball camp, and he's looking forward to some serious on-court action for two weeks straight — but Chip, his completely unserious new roommate, seems to have other ideas . . .

Fast Break
by Michael Coldwell

Meeting people in a new town is hard. So when Jeff runs into a group of guys who love basketball as much as he does, he makes sure to stick with them when school starts. But at school, he finds out what they're really like . . .

Free Throw
by Jacqueline Guest

When his mother remarries, suddenly everything changes for Matt: new school, new father, five annoying new sisters, even a smelly new dog. Worst of all, if he wants to play basketball again, he'll have to play with his old team's worst enemies.

Game Face
by Sylvia Gunnery

Jay's back in Rockets territory after playing for a rival team last year, and not everyone on the basketball team is welcoming him home. When Jay beats out former best friend and MVP Colin for team captain, the tension threatens to rip the team apart.

Hoop Magic
by Eric Howling

Orlando O'Malley has had to overcome a lot to play basketball. He's the worst shooter on the Evergreen Eagles middle school team. He can barely dribble around a cone in practice. And he's certainly the shortest. But Orlando has two special talents: a winning personality and the ability to call play-by-play almost everything that is happening around him.

Hustle
by Johnny Boateng

Johnny "Hustle" Huttle comes from an inner-city neighbourhood, where the streets are tough and the street ball games are rougher. Johnny wants to shine as the school's star basketball player, but his best friend bests him effortlessly at everything, on and off the court.

Nothing But Net
by Michael Coldwell

Playing in an out-of-town tournament can be rough, especially when you know you're the worst team on the court. But when you've got nothing to lose and a wild man like Chip Carson on your side, anything can happen . . .

Out of Bounds
by Sylvia Gunnery

As if it isn't bad enough that Jay's family home has been destroyed by fire, Jay has to switch schools — which means he has to choose between playing for the enemy, and not playing basketball at all. And he can't decide which is worse.

Personal Best
by Sylvia Gunnery

Jay finally gets to go to Basketball Nova Scotia Summer Camp, and he even gets to stay in a real dorm with his best friend, Mike. But Mike's older brother is also there, and he's not exactly acting like a good coach or a good big brother . . .

Playing Favourites
by Trevor Kew

Gavin and his friends Mido and Critter are starting high school this year, which means moving from a school with a championship-winning soccer team to a school that doesn't have a team at all. After a deal for practice time leaves Gavin running the team, he soon learns that being a good coach isn't the same as being a good player.

Rebound
by Adrienne Mercer

C.J.'s just been made captain of the basketball team — but her teammate, Debi, seems determined to make C.J. miserable. Then C.J. wakes up one morning barely able to stand up. How can she show Debi up when she can't even make it onto the court?

Replay
by Steven Sandor

Warren Chen has always dreamed of being a football star, but at 90 pounds and five feet tall, he's not exactly built like a linebacker. At first the coach is reluctant to even let him try out, but soon he sees Warren's strengths — he is small, slippery, and no one can catch him.

Slam Dunk
by Steven Barwin & Gabriel David Tick

The Raptors are going co-ed — which means that for the first time ever, there will be *girls* on the team. Mason's willing to see what these girls can do, but the other guys on the team aren't so sure about this . . .

Triple Threat
by Jacqueline Guest

When Matt's online friend, Free Throw, finally comes to Bragg Creek for a visit, the first thing they do is get a team together to compete in the summer basketball league. Unfortunately, Matt's arch-enemy has had the same idea . . .